Praise for *Strange Wisdoms of the Dead*

Allen's is poetry for goths of all ages . . . There is a long tradition of poetry dealing with the uncanny — think Keats' "La Belle Dame Sans Merci" or Coleridge's "The Rime of the Ancient Mariner" — and it's nice to see someone putting it to such use again. Allen's poems . . . do a fine job of making the human scary and the scary human.
— **Editor's Choice,** *The Philadephia Inquirer*

The literary equivalent of a Caravaggio painting, where light is bright and casts all the more shadow for its brilliance . . . Fantastical places like the REM Sleep Factory, the belly of the enigmatic Time Shark, the Gates of Hell, and even the Apocalypse itself; these and others are not dark places but places where light and darkness intermingle to cast long, clawed shadows.
— *The Pedestal Magazine*

A comprehensive Mike Allen anthology covering ten years, compiling not just his poems but his fiction and collaborations as well . . . *Strange Wisdoms of the Dead* features some of his more daring and experimental work and so you might want to check this out for that. This is a splendid collection.
— **Charles Tan,** *Fantasy Literature*

Strange Wisdoms of the Dead is an excellent overview of the poet's past ten years of writing.
— **Ellen Datlow,** *Year's Best Fantasy and Horror 2007*

PRAISE FOR *THE JOURNEY TO KAILASH*

Reader, it's brilliant . . . a handsomely designed book that brings together the very best of Mike Allen's poetry. On the surface of it, this is a collection of nightmares. Mike Allen is a Tarot-deck Devil, and the most effective of these pieces partake of the dark. That land we fear to visit in our sleep is where Mike Allen lives full time, twisting the dark to his purpose. The poems in this collection are as terrifying as they are wonderful, and I highly recommend the reading of them.

— Amal El-Mohtar, *SF Site*

A vivid journey for the reader through fantastic, often dark, stories . . . There are elements of the fantastic, elements of science fiction, even elements of surrealism all rubbing against each other. Allen manages to tie it all together, whether through a recurring image or the evocative mood of the poems. *The Journey to Kailash* is a wonderful book to accompany a pot of tea before of a smoldering fire.

— *Cleveland Poetics*

PRAISE FOR *HUNGRY CONSTELLATIONS*

The poems in Mike Allen's latest book, *Hungry Constellations*, make a rowdy, red-tinged tapestry, representing twenty years of work from one of the major creative forces in this genre. These poems are physical, expansive, and revolutionary. They are grand and dystopic. They seethe with the conflict of opposites. Allen likes the destructive side of creation as much as the emergent side. He likes dying gods, because they need to be revived or transformed. He writes about stars and legends and human beings contending with the monster-filled and glorious cosmos. He does it all with a relentless, energetic style, full of thought and invention.

— John Phillip Johnson, *Star*Line*

Praise for Mike Allen

Mike Allen demonstrates a talent for walking the knife's edge.
— **James Patrick Kelly**

These poems reach beyond the narrow, inward-focusing subject matter of so much contemporary poetry to address the hopes and fears of our modern society.
— **Jane Lindskold**

Mike Allen's poetry is sometimes amusing, often disturbing, but never disappointing. Certain passages get under your skin and call you back to read them again and again, each time to find new insights, hidden meanings whispered in allegorical phrase.
— ***Strange Horizons***

Allen is arguably the speculative poet most consistently publishing poems that delight to be read aloud . . . . they play out, in compelling ways, the central mandate of the speculative muse: "Don't confine your vision."
— **Drew Morse**

The sheer variety of contexts and approaches will insure anemotional and intellectual roller-coaster ride for the lucky reader.
— **Paul Di Filippo**

Mike Allen's poetry is awash in nifty ideas, arresting images, and diabolical whimsy.
— **Lawrence Watt-Evans**

Also by Mike Allen

Novels and Novelettes
TRAIL OF SHADOWS
THE BLACK FIRE CONCERTO
THE SKY-RIDERS (with Paul Dellinger)

Story Collections
SLOW BURN
AFTERMATH OF AN INDUSTRIAL ACCIDENT
A SINISTER QUARTET (with C. S. E. Cooney,
Amanda J. McGee, and Jessica P. Wick)
THE SPIDER TAPESTRIES
UNSEAMING

Poetry Collections
HUNGRY CONSTELLATIONS
THE JOURNEY TO KAILASH
STRANGE WISDOMS OF THE DEAD
DISTURBING MUSES

As Editor
CLOCKWORK PHOENIX 5
MYTHIC DELIRIUM: VOLUME TWO (with Anita Allen)
MYTHIC DELIRIUM (with Anita Allen)
CLOCKWORK PHOENIX 4
CLOCKWORK PHOENIX 3: NEW TALES OF BEAUTY AND STRANGENESS
CLOCKWORK PHOENIX 2: MORE TALES OF BEAUTY AND STRANGENESS
CLOCKWORK PHOENIX: TALES OF BEAUTY AND STRANGENESS
MYTHIC 2
MYTHIC

STRANGE WISDOMS
OF THE DEAD

MIKE ALLEN

BOOKS

mythicdelirium.com

Strange Wisdoms of the Dead

Copyright © 2006 by Mike Allen
Mythic Delirium Books edition copyright © 2018

Greek translations by Sonya Taaffe

Cover photo by Ilkin Quliyev. Licensed by 123RF.

Cover design copyright © 2026 by Mike Allen

ISBN-13: 978-0-9889124-9-6
ISBN-10: 0-9889124-9-X

Published by Mythic Delirium Books LLC
http://mythicdelirium.com

Our gratitude goes out to the following who because of their generosity are from now on designated as supporters of Mythic Delirium Books: Saira Ali, Cora Anderson, Anonymous, Patricia M. Cryan, Steve Dempsey, Oz Drummond, Patrick Dugan, Matthew Farrer, C. R. Fowler, Mary J. Lewis, Paul T. Muse, Jr., Shyam Nunley, Finny Pendragon, Kenneth Schneyer, and Delia Sherman.

IN MEMORY OF ELIOT, KUBRICK, LOVECRAFT, TOLKIEN & POE
WHOSE STRANGE WISDOMS MADE ME WHAT I AM

This book surveys ten years of my career in the shadows—and so many have offered me help, inspiration and support during that long march that I'm sure I can't possibly pay tribute to all who deserve it in this small space. If you don't see your name here and believe it belongs, no doubt you're correct, and I apologize. And now, my thanks to those without whom this book could not be: Anita, who shares the march with me; John Benson; Nelson Bond; Bruce Boston; Lisa Jean Bothell; Harold Bowes; Sam Dean; Paul Di Filippo; Richard Dillard; Roger Dutcher; Suzette Haden Elgin; Harlan Ellison; Jack Fisher; Janet Fox; Theodora Goss; Michael Gustie; Jennifer Helms; Vickie Holt; Mary Horton; Mardel James; Mike and Mary Jones; Marvin Kaye; Jim Kelly; Angela Kessler; Kim Knott; David C. Kopaska-Merkel; Warren Lapine; Jeanne Larsen; Drew Morse; Tim Mullins; Michael Pendragon; Tom Piccirrilli; Tim Pratt; Kathryn Rantala; Cathy Reniere; Anne Sampson; Charles Saplak; Darrell Schweitzer; Marge Simon; Bob Snare; Christina Sng; Greg Stewart; Sonya Taaffe; Daniel and Patricia Trout; Scott Urban; Sean Wallace; Ian Watson; Bud Webster; Sheila Williams; Laurel Winter; Allen Wold. And lastly, thanks to Mom and Dad, who still wonder where all this darkness comes from.

CONTENTS

I.

KRYPTA

II.

CHRESTHENTA

III.

DEINA

I

κρυπτά

KRYPTA

THE STRANGE WISDOM OF THE DEAD

A cruel joke
returned his soul (briefly)
to his body,
and he clawed words
in his coffin lid:
THE EYES OF GOD
ARE FANGED MOUTHS

THE PSYCHIC ABOVE BURRITOVILLE

i. introducción

The smell, she says, her good eye
a candle-flame flicker in a limestone cave —
the other, blue and filmy as polluted water.
Si, the smell, it's maddeningly good,
always makes my mouth water.
Her smile, full of stalagmites.

From her ceiling, wide flat masks
hang like a legion of bats,
rock softly in no breeze,
feathers dangling from their
overburdened earlobes. Her table
is stone, a carved jaguar. Its purr
rumbles deep. Through incense haze
you glimpse withered heads,
peering from her shelves through wooden disks,
and wonder, are they real or wax —
why else would they sweat so?

And infused in the heady brew,
odors of burrito and quesadilla and flan,
arroz pollo, chili con carne, and
others you can't name — *paella,*
pulpo, chorizo, cabra del diablo,
she rattles, finishing your list aloud.

My sister, she's the cook. ¿Comprende?
The card springs like a knife from
gouty fingers. *Here she is, always*
under your nose. Above illuminated script,
THE COOK, indeed she's there,
plump, aproned, brown as earth.
She bustles among infinitely receding
rows of stoves, millions of dishes
bubbling and boiling and broiling,
each one a loving recombination, a new birth,
something more than the parts that went in.
Much like you, chico, or me, she says,
smiling stalagmites. *Let's see*
what's cooking now.

ii. cartas del tarot

I warn you, *señor*, my cards are mean,
crueller than any European's, *despiadadas!*
They are creatures of Manhattan now,
but they do not forget their roots.

So who are you, *mi polluelo?*
My fingers find THE CONQUERED MAN,
bare-backed, bloodied Indian bowed
before the Spaniard's gun. We will see,
before we're done, THE CONQUISTADOR.
Will this pitiful beast ever break his ropes,
or even stand? His party, long out of favor,
see how he shrinks within THE FACTORY,
where he labors for mere pennies a year.

Why does THE DICTATOR frown,
when his medals of power glint and his club

stands taller than mountains?
¡O, qué coño! — THE KNIFE FIGHT.
Who knew your heart housed such a rebel,
Conquered One? Not you. But which
is Cutter and Cut?
In the dark, their faces can't be seen.

THE DANCING GIRL twirls her red skirt
in your past, but it's her legs you were watching, mmm?
You haven't stopped spinning, and just ahead, THE CENOTE.
But where is THE VIRGIN? A beautiful chilling swim,
so many bones beneath.
What price to gain what you'll learn here?
Fear death by water.
Or perhaps just my fee.

THE GUITAR PLAYER lies with THE WIDOWED MOTHER.
He's worse than THE DANCING GIRL.
See how he changes her grief to coins?
Her children
climb her dress like hungry ants.
¿Qué sucedío con su marido?
Will I see her husband's face
if I draw THE DISAPPEARED?
Is he someone you betrayed? What weight
a friend's life against a sure path?

And here, what you chose to chase,
THE HEADDRESS, with plumes and dangling charms
and bulging eyes, beaten gold snarl.
Does anyone believe it? Not this man, *señor*.
Here, at last, THE CONQUISTADOR,
surrounded by *carne de cadáver*,
yet how clean his blade.
Dangerous to fight him with only

a ceremonial knife. To THE TEMPLE for aid —
pray to all the gods who might care, as you must,
but who
is there left to sacrifice?

Here is how it all turns out . . . .
¡Cagate en Dios! So sorry, I know
how this new smell spoils everything.
Your face, such a frightened mask —
rápidamente, I'll hide it away,
but you must look and remember:

these awkward mounds, gaping
mouths, staring eyes. Si, señor,
I too hear the flies.
THE MASS GRAVE.
There is no need, no need, no need,
for such alarm — some come here
sooner than they wish. ¿Tan qué?
Given time, we all go.
Isn't it so sad
true cities of the dead
are so unglamourous?

iii. el altar de piedra

The questions clamor: where
have the succulent kitchen smells gone?
And also: ¿Dónde estás?
Moist green oven, the jungle
grows about you like smoke,
golden fruit like shimmering masks
dangle from the vines, tempting, taunting,
protruding pulpy tongues.

Bite us, chico, we'll bite back.
The caverns above are filled with candle flames.
Heavy treads lumber from the mountain slopes,
hungry jaguar, voice the rumble of granite,
mouth wide as a man's shoulders,
eyes scooped from stone. Other eyes,
wooden, withered hordes, regard you
from between the leaves, victims of
THE DICTATOR's iron club, or carved claws.
Blood in the runnels. Blood
between stalagmite teeth.

Run, chico, run! Her grasp is crueller
than any European's. Where
is your sacrifice? Her price
has yet to be paid.

FUNERAL PIE

An old Amish recipe, you said, but perhaps
those ingredients predate the Amish,
the new world, the old, even Christianity.

Start, if luck allows, with weary anticipation,
knead until your hope grows soft, otherwise
hammer with blows of sudden shock.
Regardless of the method, your tears

should keep the dough moist. Fill with screams,
with hair torn in frustration, splinters from the door
too hot to open as the fire burned, the regrets
that pour from unasked questions that will

never be answered. Cover it, leave it
no room to breathe, let the shell harden,
trap it inside, say your goodbyes.

Bake until warm.

THE DREAM EATERS

When a dream achieves substance and shape,
condenses from the fog that forms
our collective unconscious, starts to
quiver, stretch its limbs, open its throats
to test its many voices, it also becomes edible.

And when a dream becomes real,
there are creatures lying in wait to devour it;
sleek hard-shelled predators that hunt them;
coral-veined junkies who crave them;
perverted copper-tongued beasts
that torture them first;

sensuous satin connoisseurs
who saver them in slow dissolve;
oil-crusted misers who salt
and dry and horde them.
I learned of these things and more
the day I tasted my own dreams for the first time,

a rarest of all flukes: just as I walked
in the landscape of sleep, my body walked
as if waking; at the end of my long dark hall
I tripped over my own dream as it took shape;

and I did not know what it was
until my teeth sank in; a tiny, infant thing,

it squealed and screamed, but it smelled —
of chocolate, honey,
sweet wine, succulent meat —
no matter how it struggled, I couldn't stop
and then

I saw them, these achingly beautiful
destroyers of dreams, baring their
fangs to shrill a frustrated siren song
as I stole their meal. Now they hover
just inches away in the netherworld,
never taking their eyes from me,

shredding and chewing each new dream
as it tries to be born. I've tried to poison them
with fantasies of white purity,
I have tried to feed them too much,
bloat their bellies, slow them for the kill

And now I am trying to starve them
drive myself mad to give them no dreams at all.
And with their swelling eyes,
their lengthening claws, their widening smiles,
they sing with voices like knives:
we won't wait any longer
for the dreams to emerge from your head

THE STRIP SEARCH

The Gate said "Abandon All Hope."

I thought I'd tossed all my hope away,
but when I stepped through the Gate, it still pinged.
One of the guards slithered out of its seat,
snarling as it drew forth a wand.
C'mere, it hissed,
it seems you're still holding out hope.

Its crusted hide was a Venus landscape up close.
It brushed that cold black wand all over my skin,
put it in places I don't want to talk about.
Snaggle fangs huffed in my face:
Sir, step over here, please.

Then the strip search began.
My flesh rolled up & tossed aside for mushy sifting.
Bones X-rayed, stacked in narrow rows, marrow
sucked out, tested, spit back in.
They made me open mind, heart, soul, shook them out
like sacks of flour, panned the contents
for every nugget of twinkling hope, glistening courage;
applying lethal aerosol
to any motion that could be ascribed to love or will
or malingering dreams —
sparing only a few squirming morsels
for later snacking.

Once they were done
they made me pick up my own pieces
(I did the best I could without a mirror)
then my guard kicked me out —
with a literal kick —
sent me rolling down the path to my final destination.

I'll be honest with you, it's no picnic here.
But, my friends, I still have hope. I do.

I'm not going to tell you
where I hid it.

saecula saeculorum

By night, he clambers up the northern slope,
hands, toes, numb and bloodless,
still seeking purchase in the ice, till he reaches
the Mouth, where she waits
with eyes indifferent as a winter sky.
Her spear pierces his hollow belly,
twists to draw out his bowels
like the worm that winds around the medicine staff.
His howls fail to make the snows loosen.

By day, he trudges down the eastern slope,
skin dried till cracked, burning, bleeding;
still stumbles on raw feet over sand, till he finds
the Mouth, where she waits
with eyes relentless as a summer sky.
Her cudgel shatters his furrowed rib cage,
breaks the bowl of his skull,
reduces him to essence of meat and bone,
both eaten by the dogs that pour from her cloak.

At noon, he hews into the southern slope,
bones scarred from the effort of breaking stone;
still he carves a black tunnel through rock till he
pierces the Mouth, where she waits,
eyes flashing with a springtime storm's fury.
Her fingers clamp his spindly neck,

pull him through the crevice as the Biblical camel
was forced through the needle's eye,
smothering what survives with the weight
of centuries and mountains.

At midnight, he steals across the western slope,
knowing no effort at silence will hide his approach,
yet still stalks slow among the pines till they part
to reveal the Mouth, where she waits,
watching with eyes opaque as autumn fog.
He slumps as she straddles him, he
clutches her thighs, and she takes the knife
he gives her and opens him wide. He ebbs
into her, fills her with his life;
then she casts his broken husk aside,
her flesh taut, radiant, rejuvenated
                          for another season.

cotillion in shards

I am the Queen of Fragments, she said,
of everything unfinished and broken.
No sooner this pronouncement spoken
then her four-tiered crown slid from her head
to shatter on the palace stairs, each piece
sharp as a vorpal blade, hurled as dice
at the shocked tableau; new movements spice
the Winter Dance, as bold red colors fleece
and silk and lace. Like ice from eaves
the dancers fall, none left whole but all
still breathing, Death delayed — the ball
never to see morning. No one grieves.

une petite morte

he watched himself wither in the fire,
watched his own mouth open, heard the scream
but could not find it in himself to pity;
humming an immolation ditty, he drifted
on his bodiless way, idly wondering
what he could next set aflame; surely,
thought and spark were one, his focus
a magnifying lens, his desire tinder enough
to incinerate the coldest foundation.

impulse drew him far from the blackened
bathtub scene, his transitional statement
a job for the crime scene cleaners, memorial
in kerosene; he found a former lover's new
apartment, infected her possessions; he lingered
in photographs, blurry in the background;
he manifested in woodgrain panel patterns
as she stared into space; when she bathed
he willed the water to burn, and learned

his will could only fuel his own cremation.

BIZARREMOST BAZAAR

Third eyes, a mere five crystal coins,
although a length of those lovely
silver tentacles would surely be a fair trade —
a final bit of garnish for this crawling cloak.
Aye, madame, thank you, and the eye —
Yes, a most creative placement indeed,
an accent that winks back from the very place
the male gaze is most drawn. Madame,
my compliments . . .

        The skin here,
freshly shed from the finest of farm-spawned
salamanders — see, slip it on, how snug fits
this glove, feel the fire ball in your hand
as you crook your fingers—just take care
not to scratch, or rub your eyes . . .

           This skull,
reassembled, cleaned and spiritually cleansed
from the most exclusive of exhumed royalty's
remains—perhaps even an ancestor, venerable
sir? Certainly perfect, you must agree, for
replacing that moldering jaw and giving
your poor, exposed brain some needed protection . . .

These jars, here? Only the wealthiest
of the wealthy can afford these, or need them.
Stray souls captured in the slipstream
where Time's friction warms the astral sphere.
There is no way to tell, in this rawest form,
what these wriggling mites might have been
among the living, saints, despots, worms,
behemoths, mightiest of stars or
a thoughtless rock slowly wearing away —
but even you, my friend, must admit
the gamble is far better than ending
this existence with no soul at all . . . .

GHOSTS IN THE MACHINE

Only Hollywood has the money to blow
on technological miracles
that only Hollywood has a use for:
A TRIUMPH! IN REALISTIC! SPECTRAL EFFECTS! . . .
The crew has long since become inured,

but the lead actress has no clue, and
that's what counts.
Beneath the hot lights,
the camera records her hesitant steps,
dolly rolling silently beside her on its track.

The crew's thaumaturge has done his work,
the chalk lines on the sound stage do a little more
than mark the placement of imaginary walls.
A thumb's-up from the thaumaturge; the actress,
in time-honored Horror fashion, timidly pushes

open the door; she's reached her mark, and CUE:
the spook machine.
What a scream!
Oh, what a scream!
Give her credit, she's a pro:

when she flees,
frightened out of her mind,
with airborne undead swarming about her

howling with the fury of the damned,
she sticks to her blocking.

Harvested for period costumes
and manifestations of decay,
the ghosts mob her as she hunkers down,
still screaming. Perfect! — And CUT:
reverse the machine, suck them all away.

Watching the dailies, the director gloats:
How his rivals would kill for a take like this!
Assistants nurse the actress in her trailer;
for what she's being paid, by her next scene
she'll certainly recover.

Grateful for a competitive edge, the producer
feels Big Box Office like diamonds in her pocket,
at least this once; in a year, this new effect
will be as yesterday as typewriters,
Sylvester Stallone and CGI.

A GHOST STORY

All his life, he dreamed of fire.
The same dream, repeated,
like a record scratched
on his old phonograph, not
an antique when he bought it,
that loomed in the living room
through the decades, silent,
while he passed the days
without ripples, save those
made in the sheets as he thrashed
through sleep. Always the same:
His house, the beast he rides
but can't control, the wall,
the pain and flames. He thought
he knew how he would die, and
feared to drive. None more surprised
than he the day his heart
simply stopped. He slumped
beside his ancient phonograph,
no loved ones left alive
to mourn his loss, to wonder
at the meaning of his dream . . .

All his life, he dreamed of wind,
of air that rushed beneath his feet,
of speed, begged for a horse
when he was four, his family
too poor to ever indulge any
of his flights of sun-high fancy.
Desire for the chrome sheen
that eluded his grey, listless youth
drove him to scrimp, to save,
to starve, until his first and only
love came home one day,
with sleek lines and unmuffled
engine roar. With the wind
fighting his every move he took
the turn too fast by the house
where they found that old man,
dead for weeks, forgotten.
He fought as other hands manned
the controls. The house, the wall,
the unbearable final thrill
of engulfing flames. What high
price paid for a boy's dream?

Their ghosts stare blindly from the windows as we pass,
The old man on the east side, the young man on the west.
As they wander through the house, they do not hear
each other's footfalls.

THE ROMANTIC AGE

Polidori's nag lagged behind
the thundering stallion, spurned
as Byron spurred, a fallen god
become a demon of speed, flickering
in and out of twilit forest shadows.

The doctor watched his Lord fade,
an avatar of grace in flesh grown
ethereal, the void between them
expanding forever with distance,
the electric caress his soul craved
never to be given, that hand withdrawn
to somewhere far beneath the grave.

He thought of Padua, the ordeal ahead;
Himself a jealous shadow, his Lord
devouring the court with gestures,
enthralled women like leeches attaching
themselves to every hollow word
and casually apathetic glance.

Polidori watched his master
disappear into the dark, and thought:
How very much like a vampyre.

The shadows
of two riders
fall across
a hidden face;
she watches
from the
undergrowth,
eyes widened
with a final
sight of
ancient
parchment-
yellow eyes;
her throat
opened by teeth
like hooks;
her unused
essence drained
into the soil.
No tales will
memorialize
her lonely
encounter
with immortality.

THE UNSEELIE TREE

The Unseelie Court ("Unholy Court") solely consists of those
of the fairy-like beings which are the most ugly and evil.
—*Encyclopedia Mythica*

Barren limbs curled in agonized arches,
the Unseelie Tree seems poised to strike,
as if it's about to unwind its branches
like a spider's corpse jolted into new life,
lash out to snare the unsuspecting in its
boughs, or uproot itself and crawl away;
Sometimes, in my dreams, it does.

Yet beneath the blinding summer sun,
the Tree seems harmless, merely odd;
this husk of wood that haunts my nights
crouches beside the road, aligned in a
row with humbler trees that don't exhibit
such grotesque deformities. I reach out
to snap off a piece of curiously
curved branch; it feels dry as death between
my fingers.
                What's that I hear now?
A stirring, a whisper in the underbrush
that cloaks the roots. A watcher, perhaps,
for the Unseelie Horde, hidden in
the brambles? Just what, hidden watcher,
will you tell your Queen? The fistful

of branch I hold feels sick, unclean,
like my hand could wither if I
clutch too long. I let it fall to the grass,
walk away into the world of manicured
shrubs, growling lawnmowers, sidewalks
marked with pastel hopscotch squares.

* * *

In my dream, shrieks of laughter
ride the night wind, followed by
the twisted bodies of the Horde, blown
airborne like leaves or plastic bags,
some aloft on insect wings,
others bloated as pigs or squat as toads
still improbably straddling the unseen
current, sneering children of the clouds.

I see tumult in their midst, a howling
captive; the careening Horde suppresses
his struggles. Below, the Tree unfurls
its branches, gapes its bark, opens a ragged
round maw. The captive's screams drown
out the giggles as they lower him in,
as the limbs bend inward like a sundew's,
an anemone's.
　　　　　　I sit up in bed; the piece
broken from the Tree rolls from my startled
fingers, clatters on the hardwood floor.
In the attic, above my head, voices titter.

In my dream, I hear them whisper
through the gap beneath my bedroom
door. It's time, they say, to meet the Queen.

that strange man with the green petunias

Though I didn't hear him ring or knock,
that strange man with the green petunias
is standing in my bedroom door.

green petunia petals fall.

Flowers sickly as uranium stain
leer my way atop those yearning stalks.
How did he get in? No ring or knock,

sickly rainbeat counts the clock.

and all the doors and windows locked.
The rain that beads his ashen coat
now drips upon my bedroom floor.

beetles knock behind the walls.

Neither he nor blooms can be and yet
petals wet my cheek with dew.
My ears ring and I hear the knock

you open like a cellar door.

of beetles counting in the walls.
Legged things from the petals crawl
across my face, hunting a door.

i drip upon the bedroom floor.

That strange man whose uranium face
opens petals for a petunia kiss
lifts open my face like a cellar door.
Beneath us, the earth begins to knock.

THE CLAIRVOYANT,
BETWEEN DARK & DREAM

Impossible to sleep when your inner eyes won't close,
stare fixed and blank at the night's offerings, no matter
how filthy or banal; captive audience as strange parades
array along shifting hilltops or march through narrowing halls.

But tonight, no parades at all — nothing
but a mud-brown plain, flat to horizon and beyond,
air thick with purple and crimson, bruised meat haze,
skinned mist. Then
                            — what's this? —
gunmetal grey forms stretch the membrane of sky,
force themselves out of ether, etch themselves on air,
titanic clunking gears, stratospheric chains,
shapes of drums and beams and pipes and boilers,
hungry, crawling god-machines
city-crushing spokes slicing down
wheels to grind continents like soft clay.

But in the next instant, gone, sudden as began,
leviathan outlines scattered into dust
by down-burst winds, breaths from other gods
even more depraved; the power
in their cyclone blow
stirs up the plain below, showing you

(What are you, here?
                    Remote angel observer?
Unblinking sun engaged in single focus point?)
how the plain stirs, not solid at all:
brown flakes swirling toward Heaven,
tornado-strewn leaves —
                        closer still, and you see,
not leaves at all, but skins, withered paper shells.
Kites without tethers, they fly, expanded by
the whim of gale to crude semblances of what was.
Arms flap as if seeking purchase, mouths
gape in dried ovals, heads sway on flimsy necks
as if struggling to make sense of it all.
And the faces? Far-flung strangers?

Or are they familiar,
remnants of people you know?

You are shrinking, rising, Eye in retreat,
too distant as the leaf-like things fall away;
unable to tell, as the liquid void of real sleep
pours in, Deluge of Oblivion. No way
to ever truly know: have you glimpsed
the fate of all Fate,
                    or merely your own?

HUMPTY

"Michael. Michael, wake up."

Soft-paw caresses gently shook me awake. I crawled from the sludge of dream-sleep, my body still soaked through with the movement-suppressing drugs of slumber. I only vaguely sensed the weight upon my chest.

A long snake-like limb jabbed at my face. I jerked my head up from the pillow.

Humpty smiled, his ragged teeth like shards of broken glass. One of his serpentine arms twisted forward to scratch me under the chin. "Rise and shine," he tittered. A sickly green glow burned in place of his missing eye, blinking shut in time with his laughter.

It's my oldest childhood memory:

The bars of my crib slice a cage of shadow out of the moonlight shining through my window. The air feels thick as a pillow, wet and hot, all sound muffled, a wall of silence sealing me from my father, who's sleeping in the room across the hall; the night congealed so dense not even an insect could scuttle through its murk.

Humpty crouches over me, his button eyes and felt smile an idiot mask, his blue-striped arms coiling slowly around my throat.

I pull him off and throw him out of the crib. He makes no noise when he strikes the hardwood floor. I stand up, my hands clamping around the comforting solidity of the crib-rail, and watch my new enemy right himself.

He gets up on all fours, his spindly tubular limbs arched around his egg-shaped body like spider's legs. His face tips up to look at me, then he scurries underneath the crib. When I turn around he's climbing up the bars, his limbs coiling and uncoiling like monkeys' tails, his idiotic grin unchanged.

When he reaches the top of the rail I tear him from the bars and toss him away. Immediately he rights himself again, spider-limbs splayed around him, and ascends the bars of the crib. He's fast, but neither heavy nor strong. I throw him down, over and over and over again, each time watching as he recovers his balance and scurries back.

I don't remember how the conflict ended. I'd always assumed I was recalling a nightmare.

"It took me ages to find you."

His voice was deep, gravely, but fused with a strange whiny desperation, and it sounded as if it came from around a corner somewhere, not from the toothsome grin sparkling before me. "You should thank the Creator I've come in time."

My own voice came out a croak. "What are you going to do?"

"You didn't understand then. Why would you now?" The red glare from my alarm clock glinted off his teeth. How dangerous was he, in this new form? Could I just toss him away?

"I'm glad you came to help," I said, scanning the room. No bars etched in moonlight entrapped me. The clutter of familiar objects served to further convince me this was no dream: My guitar with both E-strings unstrung, sprawled on top of the clutter of my desk, awaiting my attention. The picture of Melissa on my beside table, trapped behind cracked glass I hadn't yet gotten around to replacing. The grinning-skull poster she gave me just last week, taped to the door that leads onto the balcony. The dirty uniform of my dreaded burger-flipping employment, strewn limp across the foot of my bed.

"Then maybe you'll listen to me?" His green eye-cavity kindled bright in anticipation.

"Yes," I said, and grabbed for him. His teeth closed around my wrist.

The morning after that endless nightmare seized me in my crib, I begged my father to get rid of the doll.

"You love that doll. You've had it since before your mother died." He glared down at me, the corners of his jaw flexing. When I grew older I would learn to recognize that tensing of his jawline as an involuntary warning, an outward sign that his annoyance had reached a dangerous edge. "If I throw it in the trash, you'll be whining for it back in another hour."

"No, Dad. It tried to hurt me."

"What?" He hunched toward me, his teeth showing as he spoke. "What bullshit are you talking?"

"It came to life. It wanted to hurt me."

"What? What did you say?" His face twisted in a rictus. He lunged. He'd boiled over so suddenly I had no chance to react, but instead of reaching for me he pulled the Humpty doll out of my crib. "You don't want this any more?" He tore an arm off the doll. It made a meek thread-popping sound as it was mutilated.

I started to wail; I hadn't yet learned not to. This only egged my father on. He was panting through his teeth, the rush of the kill taking him over.

Humpty's oval body split at the seams, and I thought I saw a yellow vapor pour out from the wound, pour into my father through his mouth, eyes, ears. A final roar of effort from my father's throat, and Humpty's white innards sprayed everywhere. I screamed.

"Won't hurt you now, will he?"

I looked up into my father's lunatic eyes. This time, he reached for me.

Humpty's teeth shattered against my skin. As wicked as they looked, they were fragile as eggshells. My hand closed on *something*, stuffing, intestines, a tongue. I sprang from the bed and pushed open the sliding doors. He'd been able to climb back over the rails of my crib; but a fall from a fifth story balcony into the traffic of Salem Boulevard, still busy even at this time of night, would certainly present my unwanted guest with a more formidable challenge. Not to mention the wind that blows so cold and hard at this height, a wind that would sweep my tiny friend into God-knew-what predicament, while I watched and cackled in delight.

But only silence and darkness greeted me beyond the balcony. Empty heat stifled the air. No half-shaded windows ogled me sleepily from across the street, no bloodstream flow of headlights washed the boulevard. I'd walked out onto a perch offering a view of a vast, empty stage. What was worse, the structure housing my apartment continued down into darkness, a featureless pillar, no other balconies or lights adorning it.

The piece of Humpty in my grip squirmed. I tossed him aside with a yell. He propped himself up on all fours in his spider-like manner, his face oriented topside. His mouth opened and closed, his gums flexing like a shark's, new teeth popping in to replace the broken ones. "Explain this," I demanded.

"I was trying to when you attacked me." He used the balcony grillwork to pull himself upright. "You are in meta-reality. The auxiliary macrocosm of the timestream you inhabit. Connected events that you would normally experience as single points along the long straight line of your existence are directly linked here, grouped into wholes through the grace of a higher dimension. We're at the heart of everything, here. And everything here, is *you*."

I barely heard him. A pall of familiarity had settled over this strange new landscape. The mottled plain I perceived far below might be nothing more than a mite's-eye view of carpet. The pillar we looked out from, and the identical ones looming to either side, nothing more than bars of a crib.

An evil shape, unimaginably huge, moved in the greater darkness, its titanic footfalls muffled by the stagnant air as it approached. Amorphous, mottled with shifting light and shadow, it towered into the gray sky. I backed away, meaning to hide, but Humpty whispered, "No! Stay. Watch."

From behind us, a burst of blue light suddenly cast the shifting form into full relief — my father, his broad bare chest, his thin sinewy arms, bulbous belly, his pinched, merciless face. He opened his mouth, a malformed moon splitting open, and an orange Jack-O-Lantern glow gushed from his throat. A horrible scream rose from behind us, as my father's phantom vomitus bored through the blue glow, and I screamed too, in recognition.

It felt like a tongue, a sand-papery cat's tongue, scouring me out from the inside.

Hollowing me out . . .

My father's demon visage hovered over me, his skull outlined in flame beneath his skin, a monstrous light over the well that was my crib. That stream of yellow spiraling out of his mouth, burrowing into me. I knew the blue shining out of me was my defense, my only way to fend him off, but I didn't know how to use it. I didn't know how.

"Good," Humpty whispered. "You remember. But do you understand?"

The stage was empty again; my father had vanished.

"Understand what? What was he doing to me?"

"You don't know, Michael? After all *you've* done?"

The temptation to hurl my tormentor off the balcony returned. I thought about how his strange flesh would feel, tearing apart underneath my grip. "You're on thin ice. I don't care what kind of little god you might be, don't try to play mystical with me. Don't talk in circles. Tell me what this is about."

Humpty curled his limbs into the grillwork of the rail. His smoldering eye-socket winked at me. "I should have known. Here inside your macrocosm, you're insulated from who you are. Here, you're what you want to be."

"You're full of shit."

"No, foam." He grinned smugly. All his teeth were restored. "So who are you, really? And whose apartment are we in?"

I knelt down to glare at this demon from my past, eyes to eye. "My name is Michael Carver. And this is my apartment. If you weren't in my head, I'd be looking down on Salem Boulevard right now."

"Wrong. This is Melissa's apartment. Or at least that's the name she gave you. If you weren't outside time-space, the view you'd see from here would be the view you had when you tipped her body out over the street."

A worm slithered inside me. Humpty casually unwound one of his arms, held out a hand as if offering change to a beggar. "Would you like me to tell you what you did to her before you pitched her into the dark?"

My fingers crooked into claws. "This is a dream, and this is a lie."

"The T-shirt you're wearing." His free hand tugged at my collar. "It belongs to Jerry Coolidge. You remember him?"

"My name is Michael Carver. I live here above Salem Boulevard. I fucking flip burgers for a living, stay home at night and try to write music. I've even sold jingles to a local auto dealership."

"You met Jerry at . . . the kind of establishment you frequent, and invited him back to your domicile, which looks nothing like this. He even agreed to the handcuffs. Then you strangled him."

I grabbed for him — his teeth gnashed, even more of them shattering — but my fingers were suddenly on fire. When I held my hand up, the slashes across my knuckles were outlined in radioactive green. They faded as I watched, the sting that accompanied them lingering a few seconds more.

"See," he said, "I'm more dangerous then you think. Just hear me out."

"No. My name is Michael Carver. These calluses on my hands

45

come from plucking guitar strings, thinking notes out loud. I would never do what you're accusing me of."

"But you do, all the time. You don't flip burgers, Michael. You work in a slaughter house. You line up turkeys' necks so that the spinning blades cut their throats. The little peeping sound they make when they die drives you absolutely ape. You couldn't even finger the first cord on a guitar neck. Carver isn't even your last name. It's what you *do*."

My insides writhed like a nest of snakes. "That's not true."

Humpty's fiery eye-socket narrowed. "Would you like it not to be true?"

What if it wasn't a dream? What if it wasn't? "Yes. Okay. How?"

"We must leave here."

Whether I was dreaming, or truly in another universe, it made sense to me to follow this homunculus from my childhood, and bring this nightmare to a quick end. And wake up to what? Fingering guitar strings above a flow of headlights, or dried blood, sweat, and a stink of death in my pores?

Strutting like a majorette, he lead me out into a featureless hallway that terminated in stairs. "They're steep," he remarked. "Be careful."

The stairs plunged in a tight spiral. Their texture gradually changed, from the rugged carpeting of my apartment complex, to the warped creaking boards of my grandfather's house, that decaying conglomeration of peeling plaster and rotting wood where my father raised me. Humpty scurried before me on all fours.

I called down to him, "Why are you helping me? I made my father shred you into pieces."

The glint of green that was his eye-socket paused in shadow. "There's no more time. Even using the shortcut of your macrocosm, I nearly found you too late." He continued his descent. "Right now, within the bounds of normal space-time, the police are on their way to your flat. And they're going to find the things you have stuffed under your bed. And they'll find what you have soaking in your bathtub."

"What do you mean? I told you I haven't done anything."

"Once they find those things, once you're caught, it's all over. Too many other time-streams mingled with yours. It won't be possible to fix what your father did."

We emerged from a portal, began a hike across the convoluted terrain of sheets and blankets. Cresting a fold, I beheld the remains of my childhood. The body I wore in infancy, a boneless shell, a shriveled egg-case. Empty eye-holes stared in wildly different directions from my collapsed face.

"He's in there," Humpty said. "Your father."

We ascended the spongy slope of one boneless cheek, lowered ourselves into the fleshy cavern of an empty eye. "He lives here now," said Humpty. "If you want to save yourself, you'll have to evict him."

"How?" No answer came. Humpty had vanished, swallowed up, it seemed, by the membranes of my childhood's hollowed-out husk. This abandonment brought only a moment's panic, quickly replaced by relief. That creature was no source of nostalgia; I was glad he'd left me.

I continued the descent, intent on bringing this ordeal to its conclusion. I clambered down through the optic nerve channel, through a heavy wooden trapdoor, into a space I assumed to be my own skull cavity. But it was my father's cluttered study, a room I'd only seen via forbidden glimpses through a keyhole while my father was still alive. The same room where he'd finally had his heart attack.

My father was seated at his desk, digging a fountain pen into a cut on his hand, using the blood to write in a book. All at once he started, looked up at me and bellowed, "What the *hell* are you doing in here?"

"This is my universe," I said. "You don't belong in it."

"The hell I don't. I created everything here, including you." He stood up.

"You scooped this out of me. You stole the life that belonged to me." I could feel the blue aura building inside me that I'd been helpless to use as a child, that I never had learned to use.

"Shut up!" Fire erupted from his mouth. Suddenly I was blind. I stumbled over something and fell, my face a mask of pain. My vision returned, blurred with agony. He stood over me, smoke streaming from his eyes, mouth radiating red from the magma heat inside him.

Blue light reflected from the polished floor, that glow coming out of me, and I was helpless, unable to strike with it, unable to comprehend how. My frustration imploded into the purest rage I've ever felt. I came roaring up, seizing the leg of the lamp table as I rose. The lamp shattered on the floor as I swung the table at my father's head. I felt the jarring impact down through my arm as it connected; then the table exploded in a burst of fire.

The force threw me against a wall. I felt a hundred splinters embed themselves. I screamed. A stack of storage crates collapsed on top of me, their weight crushing the air out of my lungs. Humpty's idiot smile leered at me, his torn-up remains spilled from one of the boxes.

I grasped one of his long cloth arms.

My father loomed over me, grinning, gloating. He opened his mouth to breathe. I hooked his ankle with mine, and sent him sprawling. He grunted like a poleaxed bear when he landed. I sprang on him before he could recover, and wrapped Humpty's arm around his throat.

He tried to blast me with a great intake of breath, but I twisted my arm-tourniquet tighter. He thrashed, his face purpling. The smoke from his eyes fizzled out, leaving only empty sockets.

Humpty's arm twitched in my grip.

I cried out, jumped back. Instead of releasing, the arm began to tighten of its own accord.

My father's face withered like paper set aflame. First smoke rose from his chest, then flickers of combustion, then a roaring fire. I scrambled to find the door, but I couldn't see for the smoke. The soot from my father's pyre filled my lungs, and the chaos of the scene darkly drifted away.

"Well, brother, I have to thank you." Humpty sat on my chest, whole again, his ruptured stitches repaired with shimmering threads of ethereal yellow, that essence I'd seen my father swallow so long ago. "You're free now. We're both free now."

We were back in my bedroom — or was it Melissa's? Mine, I decided. "You. You were my father's familiar. His magic totem. His power source." A vast shape squatted on the bed, something hunched and multi-limbed and only vaguely humanoid, formed of nothing more than pinpricks of darkness. Its convoluted anatomy corresponded with the doll's in only one place — the wide, glass-filled mouth.

"So you can see me. What I really am. You could never do that before." I felt the combined weight of his two forms squeezing out my breath. "I never enjoyed being owned. Your father was strong, as you are strong. You would not believe what I went through, to sneak a way out of your private hell, to bring you in. Now we can both leave."

"Get off me. Please."

"Your innocence has always been so delectable. I thought before that if I could claim your strength I could escape. But under your father's iron fist I was too weak. No more. No weakness now."

He began his four-limbed spider crawl toward me. The vast black shape shifted above me. I tried to throw him off, but he was too heavy.

His teeth closed around my face.

I awaken in Melissa's apartment. Mine, as well — we live together. I hear her breath rasping beside me. Her face, round and beautiful, is rendered ghoulish in the green illumination. The greenish glow is emanating from me.

I get up, go to the sliding doors that lead to the balcony, stare at my reflection in the glass. Green embers smolder in one hollow eye-socket. My own idiot smile flashes back at me.

A great form composed of darkness looms behind me, the pitch black of its presence matched only by the sudden abyss of hunger that yawns inside me, that causes me to turn to my sleeping partner with a new appreciation for her innocence.

II

χρησθέντα

CHRESTHENTA

JARS

Jazzy June-bug heat
lulls the swarming stalks
of grass, a fine night

for jars of fireflies,
flashes of brilliance
slowly suffocating.

Gravel shifts, scatters
in our wake, scatting
secret rhythms;

we step into mesquite-
scented wind, peer
into other lives,

glimpses of lamps,
curtains, ceiling tile
sketch depth behind

panes of glass
through which passes
only muffled light.

MORSE CODE

The rain begins again, soft rooftop clatter,
summoned perhaps by the flutter of an insect
wing, or maybe Mother's drumming fingers,
recorded and echoed in the creak of wood,
amplified through the cellophane of scrapbooks

and historic photo tomes. Her fingers beat
asymmetric patterns on the table, spelling out
enigmatic deep-river rhythms as she pondered
a face or a yellowed news clip before pasting
it in her private narrative with a surgeon's care,

a nightly ritual performed at the dining room
altar, where we now sit, cleaning off paper plates,
listening to the morse code of insect wings,
listening for words in the raindrop patter.

A CURTAIN OF STARS

The needle repeats
with imperfect persistence
dotted thread lines,
new meridians in cloth,

stitches connections
between constellations,
binds warm lining
to a curtain of stars

a seam that would
only compliment
the cloud-free night
should it appear there

suddenly crisscrossing
the Milky Way.
The spirits of the stars
are with us tonight

watching from the heart
of the fire; sparks rise
to the flue as you stitch
a new cosmos together.

PETTING THE TIME SHARK

An endless line of instants swims past,
interlocking scales, aimed in one direction,
a kaleidoscope of temptation; reach out,
slide your hand into the future.
Feel the flux of time against your palm,
unyielding fluid, flow of glass;
Stroke, always forward, never back,
never force your hand into the past,
lest it split, fragment, lay raw nerves
               open to history.

DEFACING THE MOON

Your ship's sharpened keel
slides across airless seas,
blown by the breath of your desires.

Those sails stretch like skin
to catch the winds of your whimsy,
and the keelblade carves crags
into cheekbones and eyes.

Soon your own face will rise
from the moon's far side,
awaken and stare down the sun.

COSMIC EGO

I kick Earth away
unbound, I'm the space-borne son
all attraction done

orbits drift astray
without me, Earth slides and slips
Newton's millstone scrapped

cackling, I adapt
coast on Kepler's ellipse
while stars dance with joy

new orbits entered
all Heaven's spheres re-centered
Aristotle's boy

who proves all Cosmos
spins at my whim: I, the soul
ruling paradigm

GODSPORE

colors tint the wind
seductive iridescence
a silk-tongued essence

tasted skin and grinned
brushed lips as might sly pollen
slid inside your cells

bloomed like coral bells
walls of self collapsed, fallen
fog of slow dissolve

unites our senses
our prism hues condense as
naked souls devolve

birthed anew as one
all-seeing I; my notions
sculpt oceans from sky

Descent into light;
I plunge through
cold blue radiance,
diving toward
bright freezing white;
My body dissolves
into this essence
of everything;
all universes
converge, here
at the freezing point
                of light —

—of night —
at the boiling point
disperse, here
all universes
of everything;
into this absence
My body disbands
black boiling night;
striving toward
warm blue dusk,
I soar through
Ascent into darkness;

PHASE SHIFT

Straining
        the limits
                of light—
                        ions flow

                                through the mesh
                                        of my
                                                flesh
Swarming in   as I
        the cockpit of
                                                gather velocity,
        my skull, minds   accumulate mass,
        direct my mind,   shout,
                                                scream,
                my veins pump to   inhale atoms,
                                                exhale fusion
                their commanding   fire, plunge
                electron   headlong
                pulse;   into the
                at their command   empty
                my jaws spread   matrix,
                wide, swallow   propel
                matter which I   myself at
                ignite,   light
                expell,   speed
        shave skin   screaming,   through
    icy knives   from my   as I   the
    my synapses,   hull,   hurtle
    overload   as I'm   through the **void**

    demands   compelled   the
                    by my masters   through
momentum—   to bear their   cargoes
pable   meaningless
stop-
Un-

MOMENTUM

61

PULSE

Red pulse black pulse blue pulse sound thrums
quantum chance rhythm beats with subatomic
possibilities that pulse up pulse down pulse with

uncountable thousands of divisions in the stream
of time pounding a music of fate beating executing
the most unlikely steps on the gallows of wave

function probability procreation and intertwining
destiny testifying for a hopeless cause resisting
the pulse is like rejecting gravity like swimming

against the undertow of infinity it's best yes
to surrender to move to the rhythm of blood
of heartbeat of breath of desire of impetus to survive

that will which existed before consciousness still
stares out from the space between atoms made
of tones composed in probability scale notes

once compressed in the mote that made the big
band bang the sound that awakened all of everything
strung the cords of existence on the bars of time

and forced the music into pulsing motion

desolvation

they met in the realm of Illions
particles of graysad slid between
spaces in their atoms
bonded with electrons
in perverse embrasion

deathwisher/she had come willing

extranged exhile/he came coerced

skinshine unyet dimmed
drew them to each other
through viscous dark
till she floted above
      around
  below him
observing silent while
he begged for release

red   from his mouth
    spilled
white   from her eyes
   substance
desolved into the illmist

darkthreads ran them both through
on subatomic scale

or same thread infinitely ricocheted

till she gasped
as his desperation billowed
into her
he screamed
at the flood of her voidlove

          and these things
     they learned about each other:

He resisted all	She resisted all
attempts at wombjar transmution	efforts to phenostabilize
born with numerous defects	at birth could polymorph
unjoined bones, an extra heart	at whim, sprout fins or fangs
multiple genitals	grow gills
black spinal cord exposed	expand them to wings
She spent her childhood	He spent his childhood
as a creature of chemicals	as a creature of surgeries
forced to ingest/inject	broken resown
restrictors and constrictors	resown broken
till elasticity gone	sometimes lifesaving measures
till she found a pusher	sometimes punishment
to filter R_x from her blood	for a mind that refused
replace with ecstasizors	all imprinting
He defied his instructors	She defied her instructors
took a labeled-masculine lover	developed a ductwork addiction
who existed	had her midriff replaced
only as an organhead	with snaky black intestubes
tethered by tubes that	lounged lamialike
held a beating heart, his	at seediest sexbars,
or someone else's;	twisted avatar of twisted lust;
deliberately allowed his guardian	forced her surmother
to catch them at intercourse	to uncoil her from lover after lover

She always felt	He always felt
formed of liquid	made from stone
impermanent puddle	ungainly golem
toxic oilslick	creature of ancient
a disdain	crumbling brick
a stain	he longed
resolved	lusted
to end her flesh	to end all flesh

AND SUPERVERSIVE POWERS
CYCLING EVER THROUGH
PNEUMATRIX LATTICE
NOTED THEIR DARKENING NODES
TAGGED THEM FOR THE
REALM OF IONILL

they learned these things about each other and more, all
festered lies, cold shames, moist embarrassment agonies
now mutual self-torture from two indistinct points of view

In their forced illunion something new breathed a moment:
angry pulsing fleshy blur radiating hate for all inside and out
thing of groping filaments, thirsty radiation, apocalyptic motive

spreading and spreading and spreading, thin, thinner, thinnest
and dissolved

        like a million other Illion-marked
        before and since

        Particles of their rebellion
        spread to the edge of
        the Ionill sphere
        pounding in futile quarkscaled rage
        against a barrier that
        noted their existence
        or did not

METAREBELLION

This is the time, the Soothspeaker said,
the webbing of her mind filled with tangles
of light, the clusters of her eyes pressed
shut. *The time to question false wisdom,
a time to know that the shackles binding
your souls do not exist for justice's sake.*

The trembling thought-strands that stretched
from her head into the walls, the vaulted ceiling,
the universe, convulsed and recoiled. Her eye
clusters writhed, her chorus of mouths howled
in agony. The Thoughtseekers had found her,
from the dark corners of time they attacked.
Lightning leapt from her synapses and
the coils of her gossamer flesh began to burn.

We fled that place of awakening on legs, wings,
on superstring strands, terrified but aware.
Some tore holes in space and leapt through,
some scattered into quantum futures, some
flashed away in ships of light, some shifted
to energy and hid in the space between atoms.

Invisible, our rebellion still spreads, planted
in a billion mindmasses clustered around
as many worlds, those billions as vulnerable,
as gullible, as we cnce were. *Do not accept,*
we whisper down the soul-webs. *Do not believe.*

APOTHEOSIS

This moment, frozen, whirls in four
dimensions — outside yourself, view it from all
possible angles, impossible angles,
your eyes rolled up in your chubby man-child
face, your body trapped in time's pause,

a tableau of frightened family members
petrified around the table, momma dropping
the serving spoon, Da spilling beer on
his coveralls, your little sister paralyzed
in a shriek. The door that opened when
the other minds touched yours, a portal
to nowhere, surrounds you in an aureole.

Dishes hang suspended in air, capsized
by the shock wave that rattled the walls —
walls that don't confine your vision,
vision that passes through decayed
timbers, through the slow water flow

of surrounding trees, through grub-filled
earth, through the smoky mass of
thunderheads above. You see your
severed, headless past; a future
of wild-eyed crowds, of rain storms
that accompany your raised fists.

You see faces filled with fear ahead,
your loved ones' faces, frozen forever;
moons of terror over a desert of darkness.
You understand that beyond this
spinning moment, everything changes.

You must prepare, say the voices from
the door's other side, while there is time.

THE BEST OF ALL PROBABLE WORLDS

So depressing it is to sit here and know
I exist in the most likely of universes: this one,
where you don't even know I exist.
But could the quantum cosmos be so

purposefully cruel? In all probability, you and I
are (as good as) wed, starting and ending our nights
in a hot sheen of sweat, shaping our dreams
and schemes every morning over coffee and eggs.

Maybe this existence is just a wave function
backwater, a sharp slide down the curve
from a universe where our lives are more cordially
entwined, where we often meet for tea and chat

and I feel no emptiness; and around some
improbable corner from the cosmos of cat and mouse
games, where we play femme fatale and
rough-hewn anti-hero, darkening pool halls

with cigarette smoke and the jealous stares
of our peers. Surely it's all much more likely
than that place of dark fate where I've caved in
to my worst, lost my cool and my reason,

unchecked by restraint or restraining order,
keeping vigil in my car outside your dingy
apartment, following you on your daily drive to work.
And impossible that somewhen, that pistol gleams

in your hand — Leave, you say, but why
the tear-stained notes slid late at night
underneath my door? Why linger at the window,
nude, when you know I'm watching you, and *him?*

Somewhere, in some other universe, you have
murdered me before I could murder you.
Perhaps the best of all probable worlds are
the many billions where we've never met at all.

HOW I WILL OUTWIT THE TIME THIEVES

at last I see this conspiracy
for what it is: a temporal embezzlement

siphoning away my time for (life) (love) (you)
into phantom accounts opened
outside the borders of event and effect

murdering thieves   piss away my
precious moments to make their own hours pass
in blueblood gourmet leisure   depriving
my days of sleep, of spark, crammed full

of phone calls and subshriek demands and meals
crammed down on the fly   while I starve
for a second of rest they lounge in their
celestial sofas with all the time in the world
to indulge their whims and fleshy one night stands
(one endless night, stolen contraband)

no   cops to take the report
no   courts to condemn the crime
no   headsman to hew off their hands
I   must scheme and plot and turn vigilant vigilante

make my own time, counterfeit the minutes,
stuff them in the cracks, pad here, pad here,
breaths of fresh air injected in the frantic

then, once I've made enough room to move
grasp a length of time with my fingers   Tie a knot

darling, I've reserved a loop   let's slip into and
spend a forgotten while   Emerge
the same moment we left, sweaty and spent
and badly in need of a shower

could I make a double knot, could our circle eat its own tail,
divide into a new stream with each choice
we make inside   the infinities together we so richly deserve
all played out even before they begin?

But where, when have you gone?   (the more
time I make, the less you have   slipping away

carried off in the stream)

whose time must we steal to have a future together?

SPACE WAR

SPACE went to war with itself at 8:20 Tuesday morning
on the phony oriental rug in my living room.

The bombardments and aftermath I sensed, in some sixth way;
everything looked/felt/smelled/sounded the same
yet an invisible encroachment, an enlarging of small,
a tightening, a suffocation of cramp, imposed itself
just beyond my skin; perhaps you didn't believe me then —
though stacks of books, mounds of paper, rows of knick-knacks
leaned closer, loomed larger, the very walls snuggling close,
cozier, leaving me short of breath, in shock and awe.

Or that's what I thought then, not understanding,
though the objects that inhabited SPACE with me did,
desperately stretching for each other, knowing they
would soon be as divided as brothers whose loyalties
lay to either side of the Mason-Dixon line.

Oh, but now, I live in No-Man's-Land, and since you left,
no woman's. The cause of this madness still lies just outside
the edge of my mind, my grasp; did LENGTH offend HEIGHT,
or HEIGHT break its truce with WIDTH, or VOLUME
volley insults at AREA? Or did the dominoes of murder
and betrayal and treaties broken begin their topple more locally:
Floor vowing vengeance on Ceiling, forcing all of Attic

to mobilize, the conflagration bending UP and NEAR
in lines I cannot fathom, every treacherous step
leading elsewhere, nowhere, following no direction,
one moment falling, another compressed
on all sides, too crushed to scream.

My rooms slip in and out of higher dimensions.
I cannot distinguish one filthy SPACE from another.
This house has balkanized, with me its single lost refugee;
nothing remains of the world I understood except nothing,
that deprivation of all, deprived even of peace.

SPACE undone in your vacuum
but TIME, tormentor, won't abandon me;
it forces forward motion, oblivious, unsleeping.
I don't know how you found the door out, but couldn't you
have shown me the way?

PSYCHOSPACE SINGULARITY

The first manifested on the Mall, in the shadow
of George Washington's spire; some schmuck
with computer in palm, cell phone in ear and
mind packed denser than matter with yellow alerts,
stocks and porn and spam and trashy pop-up ads

and plans to cheat on his second wife with his latest
gold-digger secretary and three partners in cybersex,
and plots to disappear pension funds into phantom
accounts offshore, and schemes to squirm out of child
support for his first wife's brats — that weakened mind,

crammed hyperdense, abruptly surpassed critical mass:
bypassed the nova, dived straight to psychic collapse,
creating a walking husk topped by a head full of hole —
a bottomless funnel punctured in psychospace, slurping in
nearby souls of dull-eyed tourists and federal drones

like so many unfortunate planets, blundering into
the event horizon and emerging as born-again zombies.
Between blocks he lumbered, past metro stations,
office towers, gridlocked bypasses, dragging out
stunned ghosts in droves from their machines of flesh —

spun into his head and flushed away. And he was
just the first, the sucking spark that made the center
fall apart. Soon thousands of minds puckered smaller
than nothing; millions more felt that first fatal tug
of psychotic gravity. Now no one dares enter the cities:

"Go there and you're sure to lose your mind."
We're scattered now, as far as land will allow;
settlements too thick soon are thinned. To have
neighbors is to risk stretching the well; to touch
invites oblivion. Further, further, further we spread:

the human race in the throes of heat death.

EATING THE TIME SHARK

of course, in the end, it will eat you
with unkindest of kisses
your teeth, tongue, face, brain
sliding down its endless gullet

but though it's at best uneven comfort
there is space for skilled teeth to fight the current —
room, if you're fleet enough
to dine on your own fate

the pilot fish that swims alongside
the remora that attaches and rides
the lamprey that slices and bleeds
can you be stronger, swifter, more precise than these?
braving backwash and undertow
incising forward between the instant-thin
scales of history?

then masticating crosstime,
most delicate and diverse of all meals:
savoring the steak
more like a hallucinatory scotch
than any meaty texture
a burst of primaeval mud upon the mind's palate

followed by crackle of wood igniting
feral taste of iron, copper taste of blood
grit of concrete, bubbles of steam
stickiness of plastic topped with electric prickles
and aftertaste of diesel and silicon

bite deeper, deeper yet:
can you explore
the sweetness of a forming sun
bitter nebulas
the incomprehensible flavor
of the unexploded big bang

eternally starving parasite
can you burrow your way out of time?
can you burn your self to nothing
before you're swallowed?

BETWEEN STANZAS

The boy's hair, streaked with blond highlights, curled in a designer bob just above his chin — but he insisted he was homeless. When I asked him where he stayed he glanced aside sheepishly. "I'm challenged," he said.

He wore a black three-piece suit, the coat decorated along every seam with linked chains of safety pins. He intended that to be some sort of statement against the assholery of corporate America. I confess I didn't entirely understand the minutiae of his protest.

He said his name was John, or Justice, or maybe both at different times. He came up to me during a break in the round robin poetry reading — I, continuing my role as the evening's square peg, the guy who read from a chapbook rather than reciting or inventing, stayed put in the restaurant's dim-lit "wine-cellar," while all the black-clad young men and all the bangled and sandled young women went outside to smoke.

I wasn't entirely comfortable with John-Justice's attention, but he intrigued me, so I didn't try to shoo him off.

"You're the only one here who's really putting your soul into what you write," he said. "I can tell."

I thanked him with a smile that I hoped would appear not too arrogant and not too leery. I certainly knew that, compared to the long rants against the current political regime, or the swear-word-packed invectives against religious brainwashing, or even one heartfelt, flowing screed about abuses in a dysfunctional family, my own askew phantasms had to seem rather quaint, things not at all attuned to the breeze of the moment.

My stack of humble chapbooks shifted of their own accord on the table as he leaned over me, pressing an inch or two into my personal space. His face was unlined, streamlined, somewhat fey. Had he been a woman, I might have found him quite striking, though not precisely beautiful.

He dipped his fingers into his collar, hooking a length of necklace chain and drawing it out, until the thing secretly dangling against his heart appeared in his hand.

Now he had my attention.

The object on the end of the chain fluttered, though it had no wings. It glistened with a fluid mirror sheen, its surface like spilled mercury, but nothing reflected there matched the surrounding room. In its shapelessness there were a thousand shapes. Pieces of it seemed to drift outward and bud away, becoming tiny black planets that spiraled in orbit above their parent — but no, the object in his palm was of a piece, solid as a sphere of polished night, though were there also motes swimming *within* it, particles of stolen light or more intense darkness?

Our space neither brightened nor warmed, but there was unquestionably an intensity, a radiation, coming from the thing in the boy's hand that made it hard to keep my eyes focused on it, though I did.

I stared at the object for several silent seconds. Finally, I offered him a smirk that perhaps looked mischievous, but felt to me to be shaded with a tint of wariness, even weariness.

"I gave my wife one of those," I said, quietly.

III

δεινά

DEINA

THE NIGHT WATCHMAN DREAMS HIS ROUNDS AT THE REM SLEEP FACTORY

1.

He saw himself — too slow to react —
enveloped in a death ray, reduced to grey ash,
barely a snack for the dust mop.
As he continues to observe (from some vague space
above the killing ground) his faceless attackers
sweep him on to a blueprint (a scheme of the
sub-sub basement); the particles that were once
his body vanish in the ocean of blue ink;
then They fold his prison shut (darkness/
blink) — He comes to

in the sub-sub basement (still under construction/
constriction) where the naked hoses from
the venom machine undulate leglessly along the walls.
He clutches his brow, remembering the blueprint
(so briefly brushed across) crawls until he finds
the tiny Box, the Key he must turn in the Clock
on his belt to prove he passed by.
A click, a turn,
(a choral aria loosed from its enigmatic works)
another round done.

2.

He saw himself — too slow to escape —
clamber to the top of the scaffolding, force it to topple
to land him on the other side of the Hungering Pool,
    but the Pool
outmaneuvers him, grows too fast,
pulls its far shore away so he plops in the water, into the path
of the Time Shark's distending jaws, soulless radium numbers
staring from its eyesockets as he slips
beneath its submarine bulk, finds a drain,
learns to breathe water. He emerges

From the mouth of a water fountain, in time to see
an army of Flesh Fish burst from the ventilation ducts, veins
like Man-o-War tentacles dragging beneath their bellies,
a slimy swarm gliding into the employee lounge
to claim the lives of dozens of his faceless co-workers, reduced
to gray meat in milliseconds. He locks the lounge door
(fish on the other side) and finds the tiny Box, the Key.
Faceless Investigators will soon arrive to sort the mess.
He locks the Fear Induction Vault as well, so They
won't find the body inside (he no longer remembers
who that man was, or why he murdered him.)
Another turn of the Key in the Clock
(which bleeds as he forces it in)
Another round done.

3.

He saw himself — too slow to comprehend —
peer out a long window slit to watch child-forms
caper on a beach: tall six-winged penguins with
bulbous eyes, bloated caterpillars with elephant
trunks, horses with corduroy skin — all slash-frozen

as mushroom clouds erupt on the horizon. He slams
the window shut against the blinding blast, too late: Faceless,
he gropes for the Eyewish station, pawing along the cold,
throbbing wall, pushes through a hatch that

drops him on the stony floor, eyes restored (not a moment
too soon) — a boot booms down a paper-width away.
He runs, all eight legs a piston blur, spins to face
his would-be killer, sees his own face snarling down at him.
He charges the kicking legs, whips his tail, stings, stings,
dodges the falling body — clambers onto the empty
husk of head, crawls inside — stands up, dusts off his uniform,
rubs his aching neck, limps off to find the Box and Key.
They're here, in a mirrored hall. A million times
reflected, he slides the Key in the Clock, strokes
(it makes a choking sound) wonders how many
rounds he's done tonight, how many split seconds of REM
recorded, what will he remember, retain,
if anything at all? If the Clock knows
it holds its piece.
Another round done.

4.

He saw himself — too scared to slow down —
running deeper underground, the Manager in hot pursuit —
black-robed, bald, the Manager had merely grinned
despite the blows he took, sawblade blows
to forehead, chest, a pretty "X" carved in the throat. He tried
every trick to bring the Manager down,
but despite even thumb-blinded eyes, still coming, chasing,
the threat of imminent arrival like hot breath on the nape
        of his neck.
In the Meathouse now, playing cat and mouse
among the malformed pig-sized embryos swinging on hooks

above the sloping floor; a voice, the Manager's master, CEO,
commanding from somewhere below.
Living bait, he leads the blinded Manager into the Cosmic Oven,
claws for the On button, learns to breath fire.
Out the other end, he descends

through one more door, to meet the yellowed gaze
of the CEO, who lies on a pallet, a creature of green bones,
yellow fungus eyes staring from a head like softened fruit.
Surrounded by faceless, white-robed sycophants,
the CEO commands to Stop!
He hears the voice inside his head, knows
not to look in those eyes.
He watches as his shined guardsman's shoes
ignore all desperate orders, step on the pallet,
into the bones, cave in the CEO's head like a puffball.
Confused sycophants follow like ducklings
to the tiny Box and Key, which turns in the Clock,
which (gives birth to birds)
turns the outside world open,
marks the ticker tape, says Goodbye.
Another night gone.

epilogue

He saw himself — as realization slowly dawned —
not shake his baton, blow his whistle, lift a finger,
as the grinning Rat-men climbed
from the submerged turbine shafts to seize the
bewildered sycophants, virgin-white offerings borne
away to the sub-sub basement (some for breeding/
some for feeding). The Clock on his belt
detaches, grins, pats him on the back

Good work, it says, as his back

sprouts unfeathered wings, the teeth
in his mouth lengthen, his skin reddens,
hooked talons grow from his hands, his head.
And he understands the night stretches long ahead,
and who pays his salary
and that he was the Manager
all along.

THE WINDOWS BREATHE

The windows breathe in this place, the ancient
time-thinned panes flexing out and in,
the reflections of the rooms ever shifting, slipping,
tricking your eyes, your own face unrecognizable
as you peer in the glass, vainly seeking a glimpse

of Outside.

Unseen, the eaves of this house ever howl, screaming
when the wind blows and when it slumbers;
and darkness forever ascends the stairs, rising
from the depths to snuff the lamps of any
who dare descend; ignore the sounds you hear
as you grope in the pitch black, and carefully count
the landings, or you may not find the floor you seek,

or any other.

The old timbers that form these floors
always creek, whether trod upon or not; it's best
to believe the footsteps that follow you
from room to room are merely the protests
of the house as it shifts; the hungry shuddering
groans no more than the complaints of aging wood.
Sometimes a door opens on a soft, sloping hall,
rounded, glistening, so much like a gullet.

Another trick of the eyes, perhaps; still
it may be wise to shut that door and wait,

or find another way.

Some come invited to this place; others trespass,
or so they think; some have lived here all along
and never knew it; some learn too soon or too late.
And me? I am no more than I seem, bent and shriveled,
with cataracts, quavering voice, a dodderer, a servant,
a guide to ensure your ordeal here ends no later

or sooner than it should.

THIRD SHIFT AT THE PLASTEEL SPISER FACTORY

It's not my place to speak,
I don't try, I just listen
to the spider goddess sprawled in front of me,
as she giggles to herself, clangs and hums,
exhales black smoke from pneumatic lungs;
pregnant Arachne spreads her iron legs apart
and beckons me inside the cage they form,
to perform a midwife's duty
my palms and wrists are pocked
with scabs and pinprick blisters;
My hands will burn again,
birth is imminent.

I crouch and her breath is a hiss of steam
as she vents the pain of her contractions;
her molds grind and slide apart
and her brood spills out into a bucket;
they scramble and swarm over one another,
clicking, ticking, clacking, clicking,
like a thousand Geiger counters;
some escape and scurry underneath
their mother's dripping belly.

They will march against the corpse-gnawing armies of flies. They will crush all the sweet-slurping skin-piercing flies. They will pry beneath our eyelids, rustle in our ears, nestle in our throats,

As I scoop the children up
to be weighed and counted,
venom leaks between my fingers;
they seethe up my arms, wailing, scratching;
their spinnerets spit out hot-melt threads,
silver strands of web that sear my skin;
As I shuck them into lead-lined crates,
the spiderlings dangle from my wrists,
try to catch a hot gust of air and drift away.

spin
webs
inside
our
mouths,
to find
and
stop
the
buzzing
of
the
flies.

THE INTERVIEW

"Here's the box," said the cannibal inside my TV set,
"Here's the box where I kept the heads.
I hid them underneath my bed
and laid awake at night
while they whispered with parched throats,
"'It's hot in here, give us some air.'"

Beautiful, the interviewer said,
Let's see that baby.

The cannibal bared his teeth and tapped
a lower incisor, and his rows of fangs
slide aside, his jaws yawned wide
to expose a silver-leafed music box
labeled HEADS INSIDE.

Beautiful, the interview said,
Let's open that baby.

"To open it," the cannibal said (as his left eye
swelled to fill the screen, capillaries
wormed like angry lightning strikes
around the black pit of his pupil)
"To open it, you'll have to find the key."

Find it, screeched the interviewer,
Find that damned key!

Across the cannibal's porous face
people scrambled like frightened beetles,
their shadows dark streaks on oily skin;
searching, seeking, screaming at each other
till someone emerged triumphant
from a cancerous mole. Then CUT
to a music box keyhole; a hand
clutching a key approached

as the interview cried,
Let's get that baby open!

Then commentators cut in,
a pair of talking heads
blocking the view.
"Isn't it terrible," said the anchorman.
"Yes," the weather girl replied.
"And so's our forecast for tonight."
Then they exchanged pretty smiles.

THE NIGHT GARDENERS

shapes move beneath the shroud of night;
the night gardeners crawl from the soil

to tend blooms in the hours of unlight;
cuttings and grafts, uprootings and burials,

slicing stray limbs that grope from the hedges
to preserve perfect shapes — cubes, arches;

living monuments tortured into being
by rope and blade and unbending will

perfect petal mouths plead for food,
suckle at the bodies bled for them;

reabsorption and birth amid the leaves;
a blind, teeming mass of cave-pale children

feast on the remains of the night's labors;
and the night gardeners recede beneath the earth

and wait for the new day to die

IN A PAST LIFE,
I AM A WARLOCK'S SEVERED HEAD

the down-stroke of the axe
cuts loose the lightning in my head,
and it pours out my pupils
into the lipless smile above me

(flayed from his ivory shell,
his iron bones laid bare,
my executioner screams and rusts,
dissolves in air, bursts into dust)

i roll in my basket,
propelled by blood and wrath;
i spit black thunder
at the empty sky

THE TERRIBLE BEAUTY
OF A SEVERED NECK

Learn what it means
to be enlightened,
to have no head
and still see

windpipe, arteries now roots in the Tree
whose red fluid stems grope
for light too long denied its starving leaves

trunk rises
in crimson glory;
buds
swell to flowers;
petals open, hungry beaks
begging food, liquid necks stretching
into snakes
feathered kundalini serpents
with lips of fire, coiled branches
that bare fangs and vomit the fountain
of eternal life

Headless One
let your mouth
build the needed prayer

with silent shapes;
follow the black river beneath the moon,
till its surface begins to burn;
do not stumble blind;
all our lives dangle from the limbs
of your Tree of Life.

Let the world you choose for us
bear lotus blooms
among the skulls that hang like fruit.

HOST

Unhinge my jaw and creep through —
the space in here's meant just for you, enjoy
the lymphatic pools, the verdant spinal cascades,
the porous harmonies of the polyp choir.
You expect, perhaps, to be devoured; I will not
disappoint you — but first, dare a walk along
my silver cord. Snatch at the tattered shrouds
swimming past you in the gray, gleeful playmates;
and never mind those tremors. This thing
that shudders in my constricting throat
wasn't you anyway. Now you're free as a virus
loosed in the bloodstream. Go now, go play.

MOTHER

One by one, the children
come home,
bloodied and beaten:
tusks broken,
eyestalks severed,
mouthparts twisted out of joint,
claws split, scales
peeled away.

Against my breast I
still their weeping,
slush their screams,
stitch their wounds,
toss them flapping from the parapet
to once more face
monsters in darkness.

PATRICIDE

this lion's a viper,
i'll give you proof
(with my foot)
(planted)
          (on his neck)
(i bend his limbs)
———— the wrong way
twist until they tear free
                    SEE:
    the limbless serpent
writhe
(all the ways i've fantasized —
killing you with
crowbar hammer white-hot poker
pistol (WHIPPED not SHOT)
blades large and small
to convert your
verbal eviscerations
      into genuine
crotch-to-neck lacerations)
but none of it compares to
the intimate
                brutality
of bare hands

you demand
(HONOR THY FATHER)
that tradition
      SEAL ME SHUT:
what could be more time-honored
than the old lion
slaughtered
       by
his young

this lion
is
a sacrificial lamb

DEATH OF THE FATHER

Your naked, blackened ribs
      arch overhead,
architecture
      of the grandest decay.
I stand here,
      where your heart once pulsed
and admire the symmetry
      of your remains,
the regal thrust
      of your smouldering jaw,
the once-fertile majesty
      of your flame-scoured pelvis,
the dark mysteries
      glimpsed through the fissures
of your shattered skull.
      I walk across
the former belly
      of a former god,
my footsteps hissing in the mud
      of your combusted flesh,
and marvel
      how the mountains must have shook
with your death throes,
      how the columns of your temples

must have toppled,
        cities of marble and granite
capsizing,
        fissures swallowing
the geometric groves,
        all your worshipers
following you to the last,
        into oblivion.
I, the seed of fire
        my mother planted in you—
did you know, dear Father,
        your mate hated you so?
It consumed her,
        this invisible fire
smouldering in hiding
        as you once hid her
in the billowing cloak
        of the storm,
while her weeping, terrified mother
        scoured the mountainside . . .
every kiss, caress
        every dutiful service
masked the hate
        that devoured her soul,
that created mine,
        that longed to char
your sacred flesh,
        your profane bastards,
your centuries of mistresses,
        consenting and not,
and the world you made
        to keep yourself amused.
You let her touch your heart, again, again,
        trusting fool—

Did you understand, in the end,
      what she conceived there?
As you screamed and screamed,
      did you comprehend your doom?
Flames rise from my fingertips,
      coil in my lungs,
billow from my throat
      as I breathe.
Fed by your embers,
      I roar a pillar of fire,
announce my own birth to the sky
      I will consume.

THE ELDERS

Their name tags dub them
Elders John and David, but there's
nothing elder about them:
bookends at the kitchen counter,
smooth-skinned square-jawed faces
above constricting collars,
four identical slate eyes
fix with a stare.

When we return, says Elder John,
we're going to show you a movie.

A forkful of gelatin travels quivering
to David's mouth, inside its cube
a round fruit, impaled. Drawn from
the tines through the teeth,
the soft red sucked between the gaps,
the round thing, pale as a baby's skin,
destroyed, too, this way.

Something whirls in John's eyes,
something mad as a dervish spinning
through a desert where sun never sets,
water never flows, yet still dancing,
driven by a force other than life.

Soft red on his fingers stains
the pages he now parts,
not a testament or a book of Mormon.

We're not going to leave, says Elder John.
We're going to show you a movie.

THE EYEWISH STATION

We wash your eyes out here.
So much filth in through your eyes,
doorways to the soul, yes, and think
of what's walking in, stealing
from the larder, squatting in
your most private chambers,
shitting in corners and writing on walls.
Much flows through, yes, but only
the worst stays and settles.

This is no snake oil pitch.
I know you walk in the world
feeling oily, caked in dust and mites,
that inner sensation of things crawling
so ever-present you've simply acclimated.
I know, you want to feel child-clean,
that bright kindness and innocent cruelty,
wonder rather than weary.
How I know? Because you're no different
than any other mite crawling on this earth.

So step up to our fountain of youth.
The price is easy to pay, though the spray
that dissolves your corneas exacts
its own toll. *This* is baptism by fire.

Careful whence you scream, lest we
also dissolve your tongue (deserved
though it may be.) And now, now,
you're washed and sanitized, it's time
to show you new ways to see. Here's
your pick of socket stones (in my hand,
here, I'll help.) This one, cold and smooth,
looks only backward. This one, faceted
orb, sees the future through the tint
of your desire. This one, ever spinning,
looks down into God's true eye.
More stones, for sorting
your own kind from all others,
for reflecting the moon's fire,
for transmuting sorrow to color,
and so many more.
You will have the vision
you've always wished for.

AN EVENING STROLL

Whispers slither through the wires,
conspiracies of fire
building in the humming lines
that string together marching gallows
along the roadside.

Behind the starving empty windows,
eyes put out to hide their blindness,
lives are twisted and molested
for the sake of false fronts
and cheap videotape,
grinning doors damming in
systematic tortures,
the trickledown of stress relief,
the nuclear family food chain.

The dying sun,
nearly lowered in its grave,
stains the accelerating rain
shimmering red,
a bloodfall clumsily stanched
by thirsty concrete,
cracks in asphalt like retinal veins
filling with plasma
spilled from a ruptured-heart sky.

With each hitching breath,
my soul-stuff
mists yellow in the viscous air.
Spider-headed snakes, my hands
rise to drink, mouths bared
in my wrists, gaping, gasping,
lips working futilely
to transfuse the flow
from a dimming Heaven.

AT THE END

So you heard
the end
was coming
and you hitched
on the first
winged boat
that rolled past
and you tunneled
through
liquid rock
with nothing
but your fear
for protection
and you ate
your way
through the ice
until you
found
the end
of the world
and you looked
down into
the pit
of stars
and you
jumped:

But
you didn't
count on:
the cold
the cold
the airless cold
the boiling blood
the remote
brooding angels
too self-absorbed
to shelter you
the fall
the fall
the endless fall
unbroken by
meals or tv
or sleep
and those
who're traveling
with you
ranting hate
nazis and zealots
they're here too
yes
they're here too

finale

"It will be the supreme thrill, the only one I haven't tried."
— Serial killer Albert Fish, awaiting his death by electrocution, 1936.

Today is a day to sample death,
stick your flimsy fingers in the box
to draw out one sweet after another,
nip at the flavors of blood and burning,
lap up the juice that stains your palms.

Today is a day to swallow death,
let the bone catch in your throat,
let the bleach gnaw you from inside,
fill yourself with nails and needles
until quicksilver brims in your eyes.

Today is a day to suckle death,
gnash soft teeth on that leathery teat,
the milk to wash down your treats
sour as multitudes in unmarked graves,
bitter as bodies in the tide.

Peel away the husk of grief,
that shriek of self gouged away,
clutching at the raw, useless edge;
and what remains is slicker, smoother
than the silkiest of skin; something

you can't keep your hands from,
something you crave to cover
your every inch, as welcome
a lover as the earth that parts
the cracks in the coffin.

LET THERE BE DARKNESS

The past eludes me — yet I know the future with the clarity of vivid memory. A grand contradiction in my Father's design, that remains to me a mystery . . .

A day will come when the sun's pale yellow stare starts to fill with the taint of blood.

Among the confused and tremulous hordes of mankind, amidst the endless processions of grand towers forged from metal stolen from the moon, I will walk. One knowing face, one unique being traversing the rivers of humanity that flood this world.

Unknown now: unknown when it begins. But I shall not remain unnoticed. When the time comes, I will not hide what I am.

My life, a long cycle of waiting, to make the offer I must make.

At first my words will be mere rumor, circulating among the residents of the underdepths. My message will find its way among the filthy creatures dwelling in the sewer networks deep beneath our urban blight; creatures whose only light comes from the poisons that make their eyes phosphorescent. Whispers will find the ears of the affluent and mad who seal themselves away in underworld vaults, hording treasures from every age — hiding from some real or imagined cataclysm, yet striving to hold control of the lands above.

I will wait. Through one path or another, bubbling up through the earth, my message will emerge into day's dimming light.

Those who seek me shall find me. My misshapen face — for by human eyes it is so perceived — printed in two dimensions, projected in three, shall form the center of every conversation: rotating slowly atop the great round tables where corporate councils meet, regarded in puzzlement and awe; placed on private altars and worshiped; precious oil burned, rare beasts slaughtered, even — most horrible of all — children slain to gain my favor.

Against a growing chaos, I will speak the same words, over and over, the network of technology that wraps the world in its web providing my forum. My offer, carried as pulses of light, beamed to the void and back again:

"This world is dying. Very little time remains. Soon all you've become, all you have ever dreamed of becoming, will be scoured away.

"But humanity need not perish. He who first brought you into being didn't intend for you to die with this world. Give me your fealty, ask in humility and I, as His messenger, will strive to grant your kind a second life."

Beneath the flickering light of my burning effigy, religious despots will thunder ridicule, and their followers will chant murder in the streets. Through communication channels wired straight into the heads of their desperate listeners, the rationalists and analysts will call me mad: an exploiter, a charlatan, a parasite. Yet many more, hearing whispers from shadows of memories too ancient to be understood, will know my creed for Truth.

Knowing this, despite my visions of the imminent future, my heart will fill with hope — a human sentiment, surely, gained from so many eons among them.

Is it possible, with so much of the past behind me, that I will have forgotten the hideous service mankind grants its saviors?

The sensations, so vivid: the terrors, so real. I feel them now as I will then: Rough hands roust me from a dreamless sleep, seize my wrists in crushing grips, tear at the folds of my gown; fingers twine in my tangled locks, drag me out into a moonless night. My scalp screams as the follicles tear out — black fluid covers my eyes, clogs my vision. My assailants fill my ears with angry babble; their fingernails strip my gown away, strip skin from my back, belly, breasts . . . .

Outside this frail vessel that carries my soul, a flurry of sensations: of being bound, held high in the air, bleeding; a crowd's chorus of jeers; traveling swift in a craft along an ill-made path. Descending: a shower of blows, a rough grope that ends in a cry of disgust. Ascending.

Inside this vessel, a mounting shrill of fear — knowing what I will see when my vision clears.

When my blood-crusted eyes can finally open, a terrifying vista below: the twisting neon spires of the tallest towers of man glow ethereally in the darkness, seen from the rooftop of the tallest tower of all. Painfully harsh grips keep me doubled-over, force me to my knees, dangle me head-first over the edge . . . .

But when I twist my neck, I glimpse the stars. This night, their clusters shine brighter than any stellar panorama I will ever see with these eyes. I gaze heavenward, and know my silent appeal is useless.

Beneath my terror, a sorrow blooms. Whether mankind itself chooses its final course, or a mad, misguided few, it will not be mine to know. I make no protest at their mishandling: I leave their angry accusations, their hysterical demands, their threats of violation unanswered.

The blade of light pierces me between the breasts — thrusts upward, parting the walls of my belly. My only sound — a gasp — as my body cavities empty into the abyss; a black, viscous flow baptizes the darkness beneath me.

Those who clutch this emptied vessel — who see what flows from my gutted corpse — will know then that I was never human. Even as they let my body fall, they will know.

All will feel my passing from the flesh.

My sorrows, an affectation from my time among humans, left behind with the shell I once wore. Liberated, I shall grieve no more. I — a tiny mote of nothingness, a vast discorporeal consciousness enveloping the world — will dance through the torrents of wind and weather; swim in the gulfs between atoms . . . and wait.

The energies that bound me to my body, loosed in a massive burst, detected by the instruments of my destroyers, defying analysis. Their learned ones will flounder for explanations — a reverse in polarity? A warning from God, a message from the Spirit Mother? A formation of a white hole; the opening of a wormhole?

A beacon call.

Their radiologists will marvel, their astronomers will speculate at a grand disturbance in the cosmos, a surge in background cosmic rays. They'll mutter in alarm at a tremendous dark mass discovered by their forests of radio-telescopes, appearing spontaneously at the galaxy's edge, generated from nothing, emerging from nowhere. A drifting mass of dark matter — a dark nebula, perhaps — spilled through a rift in the fabric of space?

Only my Father — aroused by my dying call; awakening for the first time after a billion human lifetimes of sleep.

Their scientists shall whisper among themselves about the missing piece of the night sky — a widening blotch along the path of the Milky Way, invisible at first to the naked eye. A strip of stars the same age — formed from a nebula parsecs wide — all dying, all winking out at once? A dense cluster of gases, propelled toward Earth by the force of the titanic black hole in the galaxy's center?

Only my Father, swimming between the stars, drawn to the planet where His daughter died.

Their priests and priestesses will offer shrill prayers — beseeching their Lords to impart the meaning of the horrendous dark shadow that swallows the night sky; blotting the stars until nothing remains but pitch black. An omen of Armageddon, a dimming of Light before the Celestial Spheres rend? The Second Coming arrived at last, the vast darkness but the underside of New Jerusalem's greater glories?

Only my Father — closer to His destination than any Earth-bound dreamer in the most twisted of nightmares could ever conceive.

Constellations, occasionally glimpsed in the black night,

wavering, fading — the stars that define them dancing around each other; shifting, merging — their shine distorted through my Father's thick corona. Auroras cavort in twilight hours — horizon-spanning fans of blazing iridescence, triggered in the ionosphere by the winds of radiation that compose my Father's breath. In midnight hours rolling waves of mad color burst across the heavens; widening, spreading, vanishing— stars flickering within them like glowing fish seen in the abyss. Moon-sized spheres like raw red suns appear suddenly, cast aside the darkness, paint the world like an open wound — then gone.

The Children of Earth will babble, scream and shriek at what they see in the night. Some will panic, hide, resort to murder, or suicide. More tragic yet, some will welcome the sights, thinking them signs of some wondrous new contact — the start of some long-await-ed dream of rapture.

But the greatest tragedy of all will be the shroud of ignorance that smothers every one of them. The Power that could have given them new life, here to end the cycle of their evolution. Those who will suffer for the murder of His daughter, doomed never to understand the cause.

When dawn ends a new moon's night, my Father's single six-lobed hand shall appear opposite the sun, a monstrous billowing deformity dwarfing that stained yellow eye. As the world spins, my Father's hand will rise in the western sky; ascending to meet the sun in the east.

Pouring from their towers, crazed masses of humanity will reach undreamed of peaks of barbarism: Men of the urban blight will parade their dismembered children and women through the streets; military engines will sweep their killing lasers through the crowds, bringing rains of blood and severed limbs; the skyscrapers that pierce the stratosphere will spill human flesh from every window, bodies piling hundreds of feet deep, those trapped beneath crushed by the sheer weight of their fellows.

But despite all supplications, despite all attempts to escape, my

Father's hand will eclipse the sun.

As my Father's fingers close, that star's golden corona will shine out between the narrowing gaps, struggling still to give light to its daughter world. Then, absorbed in His nebulous substance, the sun's light will die; the Earth, cast in darkness; and the whole of humanity will see my Father's true face.

The face of their Creator, blotting out the Cosmos.

Then the fires will come. Shockwaves from the dying sun — stellar matter loosed from my Father's fist.

The Earth's surface, purged of life, its crust cracking open, vomiting its innards into the void, turning itself inside out.

But mankind will not die.

My Father, governor of energies and forms, will bind them to their bodies. Cast out into the cold of space — blood boiling — still they will live. Buried in the molten floods, trapped inside the cooling rock, still they will live. Burned and hollowed-out shells wandering the lifeless, airless hulk of their planet, still they will live.

The energies fueling the minds and spirits of the human race bond stronger, break brighter than those of any species blessed by His intervention in their evolution.

My Father will not let His creations go to waste.

The shimmering, ragged pucker of my Father's maw will rise above the ruined Earth — so enormous no human still possessed of eyes will ever glimpse the whole of it. Then His mouth will open, and yet another behind it, and one behind that — infinite tunnel of billion-fanged mouths, receding into His star-swallowing gullet.

Yet the Earth will not be consumed.

Instead, He will draw one great breath . . . . Stripped from the planet surface, pried from the rock, snatched from space, all His creations will be drawn into Him. All the men and women and children, their bodies boiled, broken and burned, hurled through the endless procession of stellar mouths. Even the energies of the discorporated dead — from the apes whose minds first awakened to those who perished during the sun's death — drawn into the labyrinth of tunnels through Time and Space that compose my Father's pulsing veins.

And where will I be?

When He comes, I will rejoice; and when He begins His journey to a new universe, I will join Him — the humans, their writhing shapes howling, endlessly digested, reformed, digested, reformed, to fuel my Father for his travels. Their screams, to me, only music . . . Celestial Child, I will cavort through the time-streams that carry my Father's blood, delighting in the perpetual-motion machine that is my Sire.

The past eludes me — yet I know the future with the clarity of vivid memory. A grand contradiction in my Father's design, that remains to me a mystery . . . .

Each night I lie awake, pondering why He would bind me here, to play Savior to man, to offer them all the chance to evolve beyond the limits the universe has given them — yet leave me with the certain knowledge that His plan will fail.

A lesson, perhaps, that I once understood, its significance denied to me now, that will prepare me for my eons as a world-maker?

How I long for our reunion, that at long last He may enlighten me.

IV

διαύλιαι

DIAULIAI

WITH SONYA TAAFFE

ARANEA

Touched fabric twitches,
ripples, parts; your fingers twined —
colored cobweb threads

woven between us:
frail as fishes' breath, cats' steps,

strands lighter than light,
filaments of fire, stone, flesh;
patterns bind our hands

— am I moving? Or
what line tweaked tugs me into
your constellation:

laced through time, strings thrum
against our skin; pierced, beaded,

moment on moment
tattooed through the tapestries
of the selves we weave.

WITH CHRISTINA SNG

TRANSFORMATIONS

The blades are sheathed deep
into her too-young flesh, but a flex
of bloody shoulders, hips, neck
and she transforms, a girl of thorns,
urchin of the streets, into a black
cloud of dust.

The blades fall, liberated, onto
The wet alley ground. And
in her new form, she chases
the perpetrators who'd caught her
in her sleep, binding her body
to the weights of time and death.

She hears them, leaping from atom
to atom, fleeing through the wires
that wrap the city in its hive-mind,
swirling like a carousel around her.

As the rain roars down to drown her,
She spreads out her arms, wing-like,
and tilts her head to the sky, screaming
to stop time.

Frozen around her, faces and places
register moments captured in
her photographer's mind, consumed
in a single surge of memory as
she strides proudly among
the relics of her new kingdom.

Hovering just a quantum shift away,
safe (so they think) in the gap
between universes, her creators watch
this feral child-god destroy the matrix,
their cloud-forms quaking as she
sculpts her time-space prison
like so much soft clay.

They speak in panicked static bursts
and algorithmic whispers: The next
assassins must have
no flaws.

Unaware, how fast her mind is growing.
Unaware, that she can hear them.

WITH ANITA ALLEN

BLOODSPELL

Your gaze awakens me, and now the dance
renews, a rhythm driven by the chant
of pounding pulse, the cries and tears that haunt
this chamber, echo like your beating heart
within these walls. How could you know this night
would end so? You do not shy from my touch;

your cheek against my palm, your fingers touch
the lacing of my gown; their fumbling dance
loosens these satin folds. I feel the night
call me with its chill, a crimson chant
unheard for eons in this castle's heart,
this tomb that has for so long been my haunt.

What impulse drew you, frightened boy, to haunt
these crumbling halls, to seek my star-crossed touch,
end your own life? The nectar of your heart
will slake this thirst, but first, our bodies dance
in celebration of your gift, a chant
sung in our flesh to the abyss of night.

Your warm skin conjures in my mind that night—
worst of the blood-soaked memories that haunt
this unlife forced by dying wizard's chant,
revenge that bound me—my beloved's touch,
our limbs entwined, as our souls, in the dance
immortal, his life-blood warming my heart,

reviving me. Upon his weakened heart,
he swore to see me freed that very night.
Under the sun, across the moors we'd dance;
yet never he returned and still I haunt
this place, undying, longing for his touch,
and thirsting always. Now I start to chant

his name, and you, sweet one, I hear you chant
my own—does his soul swim within your heart,
his spirit flood your veins? My parched lips touch
your straining neck, a bloody kiss. That night,
that final vow, our parting words still haunt.
Will you replace him in my endless dance?

My lover, will you chant a spell this night,
empty your slowing heart, here with me haunt,
surrender to my touch and join this dance?

WITH Christina Sng

ASUNDER

The nightmares race through the lava seas,
Blood-red upon crimson, screaming rage across
The charred, flooded Earth.

You bray in sheer delight at your nemeses transformed
Into wild hell beasts. A fitting end to dreams, you say,
Through tears of laughter.

With every mad mirthful heave of your belly, new gouts
Spew from the deeps of this dying planet.
You spread your fingers, licking lips in ecstasy,

And chasms yawn in the crust to swallow the fleeing masses
Of gazelle-legged hopes, dashing slow-moving fauna
Of crystalline sorrow beneath the boulders sent tumbling

When your fingernails scrape the wall. Stone-coloured
elementals of thought and reason crumble under your gaze,
the very bedrock surging, stretching to bury them, to seal

the graves of all that matters. As you surrender to your chaos,
your madman's tears searing out your eyes, I, the source
of all your love, hopes, nightmares, die with your sight.

Night bleeds into day as the sky peels away,
Layer by layer, purging itself into the vast void
Where the vacuum purifies everything.

WITH CHARLES M. SAPLAK

STRANGE WISDOMS OF THE DEAD

ONE

John Starkey pulled a funeral shroud from one of the corpses stacked on deck, wrapped his shoulders against the chill. He bent the corpse forward to free the shroud; it stayed slightly bent at the waist, and seemed to stare at Starkey, eyes wide but without lustre, hands frozen in a gesture of clutching.

Starkey returned to the wheel of the Saint Catherine, and barely gave the corpse another glance. He was cold, he was busy. "Laying to" the one-hundred-and-forty foot sloop was ticklish, even with a full watch onboard; Starkey was the only one alive on this creaking, half-rotted vessel.

He needed to take her out the channel, and northward about three miles. There he would lash the mainsail over hard port, and the wheel over hard starboard, as close to simultaneously as possible. At nightfall he would fire the pitch and straw in the ship's hold. The burning ship would drift south with the current. Starkey would be safely aboard the dinghy he was towing, rowing back to collect his fee. The good citizens of Bliss, those not dead from The Plague, nor taken to the hills for fear of it, would see the ship burn down to the waterline, and would know that more than one hundred and seventy of their stiff, cold brethren were being sent to the next world — and so would be off the streets, with neither smell, nor raw bone, nor ichor to bedevil the living.

The city fathers would give him seventy pieces of the local coinage — two years living, come what may. But coin was only part of the reason Starkey was here . . . .

The channel behind him, Starkey turned the Saint Catherine into the northern current. He was making the maneuver more complicated than it had to be. He needed a certain amount of extra time.

He would set the rigging first, since the wheel would be easy. He already had the ragged mainsail at full trim, and had a six-to-one block rigged to take a strain on the traveler, necessary to move the massive sail himself.

He was glad he was alone. He wouldn't have to share his pay. And what he wanted to do, no one could see . . . .

He sweated with effort, despite the chill. The air began to mist over. Strange, thought Starkey. Not the right time of day for fog to form. He glanced at the surface of the water. The normal gray translucence of early winter seawater was now a crystalline blue, a blue like the glaze on porcelain. And above it, thickening fog.

It isn't right. A current from the north, with thick fog? In late afternoon, well before nightfall? Could the blue water be that warm? Nothing makes sense . . . .

But this was not the time to puzzle. He pulled the end of the block rigging over to a ratcheting windlass on the port side amidships. He had the bitter end of the rig made around the windlass, and took up a wooden pin he could use as a lever. He inserted the pin, and leaned into it.

On deck, the stacked and shrouded cargo shifted a little as the boom tensioned and began to shift.

The fo'c'sle and jib entered the fog. Wispy fingers of mist curled 'round slowly, stroking the ship.

Starkey continued to crank the windlass, taking more and more strain. The block tightened some more, and the mainsail boom complained, but continued to swing.

The wind grew, and fog slid like snakes of smoke along the deck. The rigging creaked and complained, and the windlass shivered in his hands. Through his sailor's calluses he felt that something was wrong. Damn this old condemned stack of splinters! The rigging was rotten, the mechanisms were rotten, the hull was rotten . . . .

A rogue wave from the north punched the Saint Catherine, she lurched port, and the stack of corpses shifted. One corpse tumbled to the deck, and its shroud fell open, revealing pasty skin and caked blood. Starkey had no time to think, as rigging groaned, then sang, then snapped. The mainsail boom swept the deck, and Starkey could only watch as things unfolded with unreal speed.

And then he was struck, and darkness.

TWO

Starkey knew nothing but cold: a deep, invasive chill that frosted his bones, stung his eyes, and filled his head with visions of eternal snow. He slowly realized that his eyes were open. He lay face up on the deck, staring at a torn sail that flapped soundlessly within a shroud of fog.

He tried to rise and groaned as a knife of pain sliced his temple from within. When his eyes focused again he ran fingers through his hair, and drew them back bloody. Nausea coursed through him. He remained still until it passed, his gaze falling on one of the wrapped forms stacked nearby, on a calloused and dirty hand free from the swaddling shroud.

When he could breath steadily again, he rose, this time more gingerly, and peered seaward.

He couldn't tell if it was twilight or dawn. The fog was so thick here on deck that when he held out his arms, his hands blurred in the haze.

He could see no horizon. Saint Catherine was still in the current of blue water, but there was no wind. Fog rose in columns like "sea smoke," the fog old sailors talked about encountering in the seas where Polaris was at its highest in the night skies.

And the quiet. Yes, of course there were sounds, — the ubiquitous slapping of the waves, the groaning of the ship's wooden body, the clanking of the tackle, and a distant, low creaking from far over the water which seemed to resonate in Starkey's very bones — but these sounds were hollow and muffled, as if the fog had wrapped around the world like wool.

He needed to survey the damage. Despite his throbbing head, he made his way across the fog-shrouded deck. He stumbled once on a tangle of line ripped loose from the mainsail, but kept his feet and moved aft, making mental note of each piece of standing rigging he passed, barely noticing how the fog flowed over and around the corpses on deck as a stream dances through rocks. In a minute's time, he was at the quarterdeck.

The wheel was tied over, hard starboard. He was relieved, but forced to search the mists of his own memory. When had he tied the wheel over? After the boom struck him?

So much was blank. Had the boom struck him at all? Had it come free? It was made fast now, with the mainsail over hard port. He'd heard of memory fleeing a man after such an event . . . .

No matter. He had to anchor himself in the here and now. So the ship had survived, the rigging was relatively undamaged, and the hull was as intact as could be expected. There was one last thing to check.

He went to the aft rail, and as soon as the painter, the line to which the dinghy had been tethered, came into view, Starkey could see that something was terribly wrong.

There should have been a strain on the painter as the dinghy was towed behind, but the line lay slack.

Starkey pulled it in hand over hand, and the fact that it offered no resistance confirmed his worst fear.

The painter had been a stout rope, two inches round. Starkey examined the bitter end. Broken? No, breaking lines unravel. Cut? No, cut lines showed uniform marks from a blade. These marks were strange . . . as if it had dissolved.

This was not the end of the world. The ship would drift southward with the current. Two knots current. In three or four hours the ship would run aground in the salt marsh south of Bliss, somewhere between Whitestone and Greater Saltburn.

He could torch it right there in the swamp. It would be the decent thing to do. He may have argument back at Bliss about his seventy coins, but payment was less important than having the time to do what he had come to do . . . .

He stepped carefully through the fog and torn rigging, skirting sprawling bodies. He stooped over a small, tightly wrapped form, the body of a woman, propped against the deckhouse, where he had set her hours ago. He cradled her in his arms and carried her aft and down, through the hatch into the captain's cabin, where he set her on the bed.

In the pale light which bled through the ladderwell and through the aft portholes, he examined her.

Tenderly, he pulled away her shroud.

"Mary," he said, fighting back tears.

"Mary."

He pealed the veil away from her face. Her golden hair spilled free. Her delicate features appeared flush and hale. Her eyes were closed, her expression serene — she could have been sleeping.

Starkey felt breathless. He closed his eyes, leaned over and kissed her cold, swollen lips. They had wrapped her in bedding of lavender and pennyroyal, and their herbal aroma almost, almost masked the scent of meat.

The memory of her skin against his ached in him, tortured him, like a starving man's memory of his last meal. He wanted so much — her musical laugh, her throaty whisper against his ear, the salty taste of her flesh.

Starkey undid the lace at her collar, revealing red sores which stared at him from her bosom like accusing eyes. Her flesh below the collar had become gray and black.

136

For the first time in many, many years he closed his eyes, and prayed for his very soul.

He could not bring himself to leave her. Her weight in his arms was a comfort, as it had been far too few a night. He gave himself up to sleep, and dreams, and at times it felt that Mary pulled herself closer during the night, listening to his heart as she used to do.

THREE

The sun glittered against the calm sea, its light a trillion shards of brightness.

The good gentleman, Master John Starkey, stood on the quarterdeck of a strong ship. Although he wore the fine clothes of a wealthy merchant, the deckhands didn't mutter beneath their breath as he watched over them. He'd been one of them, he had, and although he had coin now he still knew his rocks and shoals. Even the Captain nodded to him as he passed. Starkey was a man to know . . . And his pretty young wife . . . .

There was Mary on deck now, in lace and ribbons, and fine weaves which hugged her shape. She stood with her right hand on a line of fancy rigging, her fingertips delicately curled around it, not clutching it with fear, nor with the unsteadiness of the lubber. Graceful, she was . . . .

Starkey walked up behind her, reached out to put his hand upon her shoulder. She was looking at the village of Bliss, their destination, sitting as peaceful and balanced within the rocky shore as if God had just placed it there Himself, and was watching it with His all-seeing eyes.

"Is it not beautiful, my Mary?" Starkey asked. "Is it not everything I told you it would be?"

She didn't turn around, but Starkey heard her speak.

"It is good," she said. "So good to feel again."

With infinite tenderness, Starkey put a hand to her hair; stroked the wheaten gold.

And as she turned to him with closed eyes and expressionless face, Starkey noticed that the lock of hair he touched had come off, and was tangled in his fingertips.

Starkey sat bolt upright in the captain's bed, gasping.

The bed beside him was empty, although in the lamplight he could see dust, flakes of dried blood, threads of gauze from a funeral shroud — all lying in the faint impression of a slender woman.

Twisted around the fingers of his right hand was a wispy lock of blonde hair.

Starkey calmed himself, folding the nightmare into managable sections, and placing it away.

He swung his legs to the deck, gave his blood time to settle, gave his eyes time to adjust to the dim light. Everything was as it had been when he'd passed out, except that Mary was nowhere to be seen.

Had someone come in as he had slept and taken her? That thought could have filled him with shame, but instead he felt anger.

Starkey cocked his head, listened. There was a commotion on deck. People were moving around. Were these the people who had dragged Mary from his bed?

Starkey headed up the ladderwell toward the hatch which led to the quarterdeck. Moving around within the ship he could see that night had fallen. At the hatch to the main deck he steeled himself. So they had seen him entangled with Mary. Perhaps they were just waiting for him to emerge, waiting with torches, iron eyes, a lash to shred the blasphemer's back, or even a noose rigged to the yardarm.

Well, damn them all! Had these unworthy beasts laid hands on Mary . . . .

He gritted his teeth and pressed against the hatch, swinging it up and open.

The fetid below-decks air gasped out around Starkey, and was whipped away in the breeze which ran fore to aft. The fog was still there, but stars slid through patchy gaps of clear sky above the rigging. Starkey heard the infinitely familiar rhythm of water breaking against the sides of the ship.

As his eyes adjusted he made out not a howling mob with torches, but figures moving silently about the decks. A solitary lantern in the lee of the deckhouse cast long shadows, but little light. He could barely see, and almost bumped into someone not an arm's length away from him.

He peered into the darkness, and realized just what he was seeing. Lips withered back from dry teeth, lidless eyes, hands clutching as if searching for a stolen shroud.

The corpses were no longer stacked on deck, but were moving about the ship.

Fear welled in his throat like frozen blood. Something within his mind, something normally steady and equalized, pitched and yawed just as the Saint Catherine did on this dark sea. Dreams within dreams — what was real?

Immediately, he knew what he had to do. He ran to the solitary lantern, and pulled it from its sconce. Flame was reassuring. Its light and heat were natural, worldly.

And now to the pitch and straw. This ship had to burn. No, he couldn't escape, but that was no matter. This ship, and these walking things, these undead, had to burn.

He was almost at the hatch leading to his below-decks pyre when slender fingers gently, coldly, touched his arm.

He turned, and it was Mary.

Her eyes were open, but dry and unfocused. She took his face in her hands with unnatural strength and pressed her mouth to his, her cold, dry tongue against his teeth, and when he pulled way she loosed a long, rasping sigh.

"So good to feel again," she said.

She then knocked the lamp from his hand, and it rolled across the decks and disappeared overboard.

"Onward," she whispered, pulling away into darkness.

* * *

139

FOUR

A corpse — but was it right to call it that? — stood skeletally tangled in the ship's wheel like a scarecrow on its stake. As the deck rolled, the corpse flexed at the knees, stiffly, but no less rhythmically than would a living man. It clutched the spokes and rings of the ship's wheel. In the dim starlight it could have been any one of Starkey's old quartermaster friends, standing watch through the deepest part of a dark, foggy night.

The corpse slowly wound its head over its right shoulder, and the wind plucked a lock of dry, weedy hair to one side, like an invisible hand drawing aside a curtain, showing Starkey a face of split skin and empty eye sockets.

"It is right that he should be there," said someone behind Starkey.

Starkey turned on his heel.

A man, a dead man, stood there, stiffly trying to stay still on the rolling deck, closely examining a rust-encrusted, but still sharply pointed, iron rod.

"Is this my sword?" the corpse asked.

"That's a marlinspike," Starkey said. "We use it to weave lines. Why do you say it's right that he should be there?"

"For he was a sailor," the dead man answered, not looking up from the marlinspike.

"Am I dead?" Starkey asked.

"He remembers. Or something about him remembers. He went back to the ship's wheel. He was a sailor." As he spoke he held the marlinspike before him, making stiff hacking motions, parrying motions, as if it were a sword.

"Where is my shield?" the man asked. "And where did you put my chain mail? And my helmet?"

"I've never seen those things," Starkey said. "Maybe the people who brought you in took those things away. Anything of value . . . ."

"I want to meet The Christ dressed correctly. I picture myself kneeling before God, holding my sword before me . . . . The people

140

who brought me in?"

"Do you remember being sick at all?" Starkey asked.

"I was on Pilgrimage. I was headed to Jerusalem. There was a village, not much of a place. A tiny dot by the sea. 'Bliss,' it was so named. I got sick near there. Fever. And blood."

"Am I dead?" Starkey asked again.

"What are you?" the knight asked, looking up from the corroded marlinspike, squinting at Starkey as if looking at a living man was too bright a sight for his dead eyes. "What were you?"

"Are we headed to God?" Starkey asked.

"We are headed where we are headed," the knight answered. "I'll prepare myself. You simply prepare to fire the ship."

"Why do you want the ship to burn?" Starkey asked.

The knight shrugged. "The hero is put to sea in a burning ship. He crosses over to the other side through the flames, and there I'll be greeted by God. That's what I've always dreamed of. Of course, I didn't expect to have to coordinate all of this myself."

"I'll start the fire," Starkey said. "I just need to find someone first. You can rely on me."

The knight nodded.

"God relies on you, Starkey."

FIVE

Starkey finally fired a torch. It was difficult; no hearth was burning on the ship, no cook's stove, no smith's forge. Yes, he'd scrounged flint and iron, but all the torches were damp from the infernal fog.

Starkey prowled the decks as the night wore on, his torch held high. The raised dead moved about, most in stoney silence. Some worked the rigging, others manned the rails. Some clutched their shrouds, others were naked and glistening with the fog.

Starkey went first to the quarterdeck. A figure sat there, hunched over in the darkness, its hands rhythmically moving amidst a tangle of cloth.

"Mary?" Starkey called.

The figure didn't look up.

Starkey walked to a spot over the right shoulder of the figure. The dim light of his torch revealed boney hands moving like spiders amidst a tangle of threads, tying knots, pulling bitter ends, looping bights.

"Weaver," Starkey said, "I look for a young woman. Mary is her name."

The "weaver" slowly turned her head. Her eyes were cavernous, and the dim torch found no irises to illuminate.

And then the weaver spoke, a voice as dry and distant as a desert of ice.

"Look for her here," the weaver hissed, tapping the cloth before her with a cracked and yellow finger nail.

Starkey peered at the cloth, a half-completed tapestry. He could see where parts of the sails, parts of rags left onboard the ship, parts of shrouds from the corpses themselves were being broken into their component threads then reborn into this knotted world of gray and blood-brown.

Tiny figures danced across the shroud, hand in hand with humorlessly grinning skeletons.

"This is where we all end up," the weaver said.

Starkey turned away. He had no time for these philosophies. He needed Mary — where had she gone?

Starkey padded up toward the deckhouse. Perhaps she was there, sheltered from the fog and spray. Starkey held his torch high with his right hand while he opened the aft hatch of the deckhouse with his left.

The deckhouse was still as empty as when the salvers and looters had left it, but someone was sitting on the roughhewn bench along the starboard bulkhead. Starkey knew immediately that it wasn't Mary.

When he had died he had been an old man, with wispy white hair on his temples, a bald and spotted pate, and jaws left slack by absent teeth. He sat and rocked and mumbled to himself.

Starkey didn't even consider asking this man about Mary. He proceeded toward the forward hatch of the deckhouse, edging past the mumbler, loath that he should try to reach and touch him. As he passed him he could make out the man's words:

"Whilst I traveled to my master's house I stopped and here I rest; whilst I traveled to my master's house I stopped and here I rest; whilst I traveled . . . ."

But Starkey also heard something else, something separate from the whispers of the sea and the creaking which had grown to a dull and constant rumble like distant thunder. Not the calls of dolphins nor whales, nor any other sea creature . . . . There was a feminine voice, coming from beneath a hatch which led from the deckhouse to the main hold.

Starkey raised the hatch, and, without hesitation, descended into the hold. The air there was stale and cold. He could smell the pitch and coal tar. He'd have to be careful with the torch. As he made his way amongst the bales of hay and the molded stanchions and beams, the feminine voice, mouthing things he couldn't immediately understand, led him like an invisible cord unwound within a maze.

And then he was upon them.

Normally the sight of a man between a woman's legs, pumping away, would be exciting and devious, or at the least, humorous.

But these two . . . .

The man was rhythmic in his movements, but awkward. It was as if he knew what he was doing and how to do it, but could not remember why.

The woman bleated occasionally, but her voice was dry, passionless.

"I almost felt that . . . ," she hissed into the man's ear.

Disgusted, Starkey left them behind, climbed up the ladderwell out of the hold.

Mary. All things were Mary. He needed her. Would she have returned to the captain's cabin? He hurried there.

He paused outside the captain's cabin. Lamplight shone around the edges of the hatch. Someone within moved around.

He hesitated. Would he see lovers there? Would one of them be Mary? Mary, bleating and moaning beneath some rutting carrion? He couldn't bear the thought . . . .

He decided that if he saw that, he'd fire the ship right away. And he'd hang himself before he watched it burn. He wouldn't even have to think.

Armed with that resolve, he swung open the hatch.

There were no lovers there, but a man hunched over the chart table. As the hatch opened he glanced up at Starkey. The man had arranged his shroud into a dignified cloak. He was bearded, with reddened eyes, dark grey lips, a prominent, furrowed brow.

A chart was stretched across the table. In the man's hands were dividers fashioned from sharpened finger bones, and a straightedge made from a thighbone ground and jointed down on one side.

The man only watched Starkey for a moment, then went back to work on the chart.

Starkey started to chuckle.

"Is there something you want to share?" the man asked, quietly.

"You're using our known course and speed to chart our position?" Starkey asked.

"Yes," the man answered.

"I believe we call that 'dead' reckoning," Starkey said, grinning.

The man gave no indication that he found it funny, or even understood what Starkey was talking about. He shrugged and went back to the chart.

"Where are we?" Starkey asked. "Why are we here? Who set this course?"

The bearded man smiled. As he spoke he took up a sharpened bone, and dipped it into a jagged bowl made of bone, and drew on the stretched parchment on the chart table before him.

"You question carries its own shadow. What about you, John Starkey? Think of yourself as a ship. Your life as an ocean. Where did you go and why? Did you set your own course? Were you driven?

144

Did you drift?"

As he spoke he scratched the bone splinter around the surface of the parchment, describing a lazy curve which spiraled inward.

"My life?" Starkey asked. "Short. But relentlessly long, too, day by day. I rarely had enough to eat. When the Black Death began mowing the countryside down, I was too tired to care to lower my head. Now all I want is a woman named Mary. I don't have time for your riddles. If you know where she'd be, tell me. If not, I'll leave you to draw your snail shells."

The bearded man smiled. "You don't understand this? So many things I didn't understand. I thought the stars were points on a dome above the plain of the sea. Now I can hear the whispers of green creatures who walk the shores of orange seas under blue suns. I can look at a dot of light in the night sky and see a 'snail's shell' made of millions of suns. Do you know why I draw this spiral? Look at this."

He took up the parchment and then reached back onto the captain's bed to take up a skull. He brought the two things together, wrapping the skull with the parchment.

"See this curve, this spiral? It's a loxodrome, John Starkey. The chart is flat, but the sea enwraps a round world, a sphere. Does not a ship's sail disappear over the horizon after her hull? And this loxodrome straightens out, as our course. Oh, so many things I've gained, so many things to understand, and such a short time."

Starkey noticed that the chart bore a traditional compass rose. A nice touch. But when Starkey looked closer, he saw that the compass rose was a tattoo, and the parchment of the chart was really skin.

"What were you in life?" he asked. "A butcher?"

The "navigator" laughed, pulled the chart away, and turned the skull so that Starkey could see the face. The skull still had eyes, which were whole and aware. They focused on Starkey and he recoiled.

"He serves now as he did in life," the navigator said. "It is right that he should be here."

"I leave you to your blood and riddles," Starkey said. He was almost out the hatch when the bearded man called after him.

"Riddles, Starkey? A riddle thus: 'Where is the most beautiful woman onboard a ship usually located?'"

SIX

She stood before him at the eyes of the ship, balanced and delicate, only holding the rigging with her slightly curled fingertips, standing without fear or unsteadiness, peering into the mists ahead. The skies ahead seemed to be lightening, as if with the approach of dawn. The sound which Starkey had earlier considered as a distant creaking or rumble was now a distinct thing, a maelstrom of breaking waves, yet muffled, strange in its timbre.

The wooden figurehead was gone, taken by the salvers before Saint Catherine had left port on her funerary mission. Working now as an effigy before some shop, or gracing some tavern. Now Mary had taken her place, looking for all the world like the real Saint Catherine, beautiful and grace-laden, yet bloody and broken at the wheel . . . .

Starkey set his torch in a socket for a belaying pin, and approached her.

"Mary, we're headed North. We'll fall off the ends of the Earth. These dead things. They're taking us to Hell. I'm going to fire the ship, Mary. I want you in my arms as it burns. Fire will cleanse us."

Mary glanced back at him briefly. She was smiling.

"An old ship, but a strong one, John. Old and strong, like you. It served its purpose. Be still, and take your place in the sails. Be still for the journey."

"I was more than a deckape, Mary. I had skills. Many a day I spent hours onboard some ship, earning my keep, at work on the sails, nothing there but myself, a biscuit, and a needle."

"No one doubts you, Bonnie John Starkey. You were a good man. But why would that world have a good man in it?"

But stop for a moment. Something that he said. Myself and a

biscuit. When had he eaten last? Did he feel hungry? Why didn't he feel hungry?

He couldn't be distracted. Mary stood there, idly tasting her fingertips, looking forward.

Cold. He was so cold. He breathed out to see the puff of breath he knew would come in the cold. But there was no breath visible. Mary was talking to him, but no breath was visible from her lips. It occurred to Starkey that he had seen no breath from anyone onboard. Yet it was so cold!

"Mary," he called. "I just want to be with you. I realize now what a terrible mistake it was."

"What was a mistake?"

"Everything. Everything which wasn't taking me to you. Every moment I spent away from you."

"She loved you, John Starkey," Mary said, turning to look forward, her eyes scouring the mists like a lookout.

"Who do you speak of? 'She' who? Mary, talk to me!"

She turned again to speak to him, as if he were a child demanding attention.

"It's behind us. It shrinks in importance. You want to be with me. That want is an echo, an illusion. You don't want for anything. Forget."

Her face brightened as she heard something in the distance. "It's closer, now, John! It's closer!"

John Starkey moved carefully. He needed to keep his footing. He looked down at his bare feet stepping along the rough planking of the deck. He couldn't feel the wood on the skin of his bare soles.

Finally he was beside her. He reached out to wrap his arms around her, pull her against him. He would close his eyes and not let her go, and think of nothing but her warmth and softness against him.

But she eluded him, and stepped out on the bowsprit. "Alone, John Starkey. Each alone. I don't remember," she called. The rumbling in the distance intensified, as if to punctuate her thought.

He didn't want to step out after her. He couldn't feel his feet or legs, and was sure that he would fall, or worse, knock her off into the ocean below. They would never be reunited.

He tugged at his hair. There had been blood. There had been blood before, but now there was dry, brown powder.

"Why did you leave me?" he cried.

"Now? On the ship? Or when she was alive?" Mary said.

She didn't turn around, but continued to strain forward, into the mists, from which the grinding sound was now constant.

"We each must be alone," she continued. "I can't even feel close to the one inside me."

Starkey watched her casually gesture toward her belly.

"Inside you?" Starkey mumbled, stepping forward onto the bowsprit.

"The child was yours," Mary said, then jabbed a finger forward, pointing, her eyes wide.

"Closer, it's closer!" she screamed. "There! There it is!"

SEVEN

Mists parted before the Saint Catherine. Starkey realized what he was seeing, and all the great moments of his past — when as a child he had first noticed the beating of his own heart, when he had crossed the equator and seen coal-black men and strange constellations, when he had first looked into the blue coolness of Mary's eyes — these moments faded like shadows eaten by the fall of night.

Within the mists — and he was at the very source of mist and winds and strange currents, he knew that — fog and rain themselves were the very breath of this thing he was seeing — here was an island of ice. Waves broke against its crystalline shores, ran back to the sea in howling rivulets. Sections of shore calved away and formed ice floes even as Starkey watched.

And even as the shore deteriorated beneath the onslaught of the waves it instantly rebuilt itself; the all-encompassing cold of the thing took the seawater and froze it into arches, bridges, and delicate spires, decorations in a wild landscape.

The sun — or some great light — had topped the horizon behind the castle, so that its rays shone through the ice, splitting into trillions of shards of brightness and color.

As wondrous as was the island itself, most amazing was what Starkey saw there in the island's center. A castle of sheer ice, thousands of feet tall, greater than any cathedral, greater than any city, dominated the island. And yet . . . .

Any castle was a structure, an arrangement, a static stack of stone and beams and earthenworks, existing as is. This was no dead, static structure. Even as Starkey watched the castle constructed itself, pumping the icey seawater upward through great capillaries. Far overhead, seawater was expelled in huge spouts, freezing into gracefully curved walls and ramparts and castellations.

So many details Starkey couldn't recognize in the distance. For a moment he thought this castle to be ringed around with gargoyles of ice, then he thought these figures were human bodies, washed clean of their faces, and then he saw these bodies writhing. He couldn't be sure what he was seeing. The castle was so far beyond the measure of his mind, no details were apprehensible.

Behind John Starkey, all came forward.

Corpses abandoned their places at the rails and in the rigging; the skeleton who had held the wheel tottered forward; the couple Starkey had observed humping in the hold were no longer intertwined, but stumbled forward separately.

The mumbling man was in the crowd, toothlessly mouthing, "Master, Master!"

The weaver attempted to tie her tapestry of a Danse Macabre to some standing rigging, to fly it like a battle flag.

The navigator had some instrument like an astrolabe rigged from bones, and through this he sighted the castle, noting its dimensions.

And there was the knight, bedecked in armor and helmet scrounged from bones. He still held the marlinspike; as Starkey watched he stepped to the rail, shouting, "I'm ready for Thee!" He then leapt overboard and disappeared beneath the ice and waves.

Starkey grabbed the torch from the socket where he'd set it. He had to fire the ship. That he knew. He touched the flames to the rails, the deck, to everything he could reach, but no fire would start.

"Is it not beautiful, my love? Is it not everything I told you it would be?" Mary, her face decorated with geometric webs of frost, hissed into his ear.

No fire would start. The ship lurched beneath his feet, and ice and blue water spilled onto the deck. The castle and its island were expanding, reaching forward, encompassing the Saint Catherine — a harbor of ice moving toward the ship.

Snow and mist and freezing rain fell on all like the breath of a mysterious god, and ice began to cover all.

Sprawling, slipping, Starkey dropped the torch, and desperately reached for Mary.

There she stood. All was becoming dark. Starkey felt nothing.

Supreme effort, and Starkey's fingertips touched Mary's hand.

She glanced at him. There she was.

Above all, a yawning chasm. The Saint Catherine was drawn into the castle.

Darkness completed itself.

His fingers were touching Mary.

There was nothing else.

For precious seconds, eons, he was touching her.

Then, finally, that touch also disappeared.

PUBLICATION HISTORY

"The Strange Wisdom of the Dead," original title "His True Epitaph," first appeared in *Penny Dreadful*, Winter 1998.

"The Psychic Above Burritoville" first appeared in *Jabberwocky 2*, ed. Sean Wallace, Prime Books, 2006.

"Funeral Pie" first appeared in *The Magazine of Speculative Poetry*, Spring 2002.

"The Dream Eaters" performed for stage at Mill Mountain Theatre, Waldron Stage, Roanoke, Va., March 11, 2005. First print appearance here.

"The Strip Search" performed for stage at Mill Mountain Theatre, Waldron Stage, Roanoke, Va., April 15, 2005. First print appearance in *Strange Horzions*, Oct. 3, 2005.

"saecula saeculorum," first appearance here.

"cotillion in shards," first appearance here.

"une petite morte," first appearance here.

"Bizarremost Bazaar" first appeared in *Weird Tales* #333, Sept./Oct. 2003.

"Ghosts in the Machine" first appeared in *H.P. Lovecraft's Magazine of Horror* #2, Spring 2005.

"A Ghost Story" first appeared in *Weird Tales* #327, Spring 2002.

"The Romantic Age" first appeared in *Dreams of Decadence* #2, Spring/Summer 1996.

"The Unseelie Tree" first appeared in *Petting the Time Shark*, DNA Publications, 2003.

"that strange man with the green petunias," first appearance here.

"The Clairvoyant, Between Dark and Dream" first appeared in *Jabberwocky*, ed. Sean Wallace, Prime Books, 2005.

"Humpty" first appeared in *Flesh & Blood* #9, 2002.

"Jars" first appeared in *Curbside Review*, Aug. 2002.

"Morse Code" first appeared in *Santa Clara Review*, Spring/Summer 2005.

"A Curtain of Stars" first appeared in *Star*Line* 25.5, Sept./Oct. 2002

"Cosmic Ego" first appeared in *Asimov's Science Fiction*, Dec. 2005.

"Godspore," first appearance here.

"Petting the Time Shark" first appeared in *Tales of the Unanticipated* #23, April 2002.

"Defacing the Moon" first appeared in *Scavenger's Newsletter* #160, June 1997.

"Phase Shift" first appeared in *Tales of the Unanticipated* #17, Winter 1997.

"Momentum" first appeared in *Tales of the Unanticipated* #16, Spring 1996.

"Pulse" first appeared in *Strange Horizons*, Sept. 22, 2003.

"desolvation" first appeared in *Star*Line* 28.4, July/Aug. 2005.

"Apotheosis" first appeared in *Star*Line* 26.2, March/April 2003.

"Metarebellion" first appeared in *Strange Horizons*, Nov. 4, 2004.

"The Best of All Probable Worlds" first appeared in *Dreams and Nightmares* #66, March 2004.

"How I Will Outwit the Time Thieves" first appeared in *Strange Horizons*, Dec. 22, 2003.

"Space War" first appeared in *Strange Horizons*, June 14, 2004.

"Psychospace Singularity," first appearance here.

"Eating the Time Shark," first appearance here.

"Between Stanzas," first appearance here.

"The Night Watchman Dreams His Rounds at the REM Sleep Factory" first appeared in *Dreams and Nightmares* #69, Dec. 2004.

"The Windows Breathe" first appeared in *Dreams and Nightmares* #67, June 2004.

"Third Shift at the Plasteel Spider Factory" first appeared in *Malevolence* #3, Aug. 1996.

"The Interview" first appeared in *Malevolence* #3, Aug. 1996.

"The Night Gardeners" first appeared in *Star*Line* 28.1, Jan./Feb. 2005.

"In a Past Life, I am a Warlock's Severed Head" first appeared in *Heliocentric Net* 4.3, Summer 1995.

"The Terrible Beauty of a Severed Neck" first appeared in *Star*Line* 28.5, Sept./Oct. 2005.

"Host" first appeared in *frisson* #11, Autumn 1998.

"Mother" first appeared in *Epitaph* #3, 1997.

"Patricide" first appeared in *Malevolence* #7, Winter 1998.

"Death of the Father" first appeared in *Petting the Time Shark*, DNA Publications, 2003.

About the Author

Mike Allen writes spooky things — a *Publishers Weekly* reviewer once called his stories "nightmare fuel." Two of his collections of horror tales, *Unseaming* and *Aftermath of an Industrial Accident*, were nominees for the Shirley Jackson Award, and his most recent novel, *Trail of Shadows*, won the Webster Award honoring books by Virginia writers. His other books include the collections *Slow Burn* and *The Spider Tapestries* and novel *The Black Fire Concerto*. His stories and poems have appeared in *Artemis*, *Asimov's Science Fiction*, *Apex Magazine*, *Beneath Ceaseless Skies*, *Best Horror of the Year*, *Interzone*, *Nebula Awards Showcase*, *Storyteller: A Tanith Lee Tribute Anthology*, *Strange Horizons*, *Weird Tales*, and more. His horror tale "The Button Bin" was a Nebula Award finalist. With his wife Anita, he runs Mythic Delirium Books LLC in Roanoke, Virginia. As an editor and publisher, Mike has twice been a finalist for the World Fantasy Award. Follow him on Instagram/Threads @mythicdelirium and Bluesky @mythicdelirium.bsky.social.

www.ingramcontent.com/pod-product-compliance
Lightning Source LLC
Chambersburg PA
CBHW051303250626
47155CB00009B/3407